DIVISION MANEUVER

—TWIN STAR HEROES—
SECOND DRAG RIDE

Calling her frame's new name, one half of the heroic duo dropped onto a battlefield teeming with monsters from another world.

"Argh, Kuon-kun!"

"S-sorry..."

Hanabi snorted. Kuon hastily got on his knees on top of the chair, trying to make up for his failure. They had to do this properly. Hanabi's hands reached out, cupping his cheeks. Kuon didn't dare move.

She kissed him gently.

It was Suzuka Hanabi.
He didn't ask why she
was here. He was just
glad to see her again.

CONTENTS

SHIPPO SENOO PRESENTS
DIVISION MANEUVER

DIVISION MANEUVER

VOLUME 2

STORY BY

Shippo Senoo

ILLUSTRATED BY

Nidy-2D-

Seven Seas

Seven Seas Entertainment

DIVISION MANEUVER VOL. 2 - THE TWIN STAR HEROES

© Shippo Senoo 2017
Cover illustration by Nidy-2D-

First published in Japan in 2017 by Kodansha Ltd., Tokyo.
Publication rights for this English edition arranged through
Kodansha Ltd., Tokyo.

Seven Seas press and purchase enquiries can be sent to
Marketing Manager Lianne Sentar at press@gomanga.com.
Information requiring the distribution and purchase of
digital editions is available from Digital Manager CK Russell
at digital@gomanga.com.

Follow Seven Seas Entertainment online at
sevenseasentertainment.com.

TRANSLATION: Andrew Cunningham
ADAPTATION: Dayna Abel
COVER DESIGN: KC Fabellon
INTERIOR LAYOUT & DESIGN: Clay Gardner
PROOFREADER: Jade Gardner, Stephanie Cohen
LIGHT NOVEL EDITOR: Nibedita Sen
MANAGING EDITOR: Julie Davis
EDITOR-IN-CHIEF: Adam Arnold
PUBLISHER: Jason DeAngelis

ISBN: 978-1-64275-059-1
Printed in Canada
First Printing: August 2019
10 9 8 7 6 5 4 3 2 1

A MONTH HAD PASSED since the Twin Star Heroes eliminated the Gate over the Imperial Capital.

_/////////Г

"Combat altitude of 20,000 meters achieved. Magic output at max. Systems green. Initiating contact."

In darkness, a woman in a visor read out the information displayed on her vision.

She wore a tight plugsuit beneath the red exo-armor, and both she and the armor were fixed in place. She normally kept her hair in a ponytail, but now it was wound up in a bun to keep it out of her way.

"Contact complete. Heavy Magic Engine responsive. Proceeding to final initialization sequence."

In response to her voice, a stream of red letters flowed across her visor. She'd trained for this. All was well. She was fine.

No mistakes. She could do this. Not the time to lose her nerve. Stay strong. Yet no matter how many times she told herself that, her hands wouldn't stop shaking.

Then she heard a beep. A window appeared at the lower right of her vision that read INCOMING TRANSMISSION. She opened it with thought control.

"Senpai, are you okay?"

It was him. He'd been concerned and called her. She was so happy she could dance, but she was in the middle of an operation. She had to be careful to keep her glee from overflowing. "Yeah, I'm fine. Going on ahead."

"Be careful."

A simple exchange, but she could feel herself unclenching. The muscles she'd been straining relaxed. "Thank you. I love you."

"You, too."

As he answered, the floor opened up and light spilled out in front of her. The wall of white clouds outside flowed quickly downward. Beyond them, she caught a glimpse of sunlight reflecting off the ocean's surface.

She and the mobile weapon she wore were suspended face down in the storage deck at the bottom of a ship flying 20,000 meters above the surface, preparing to drop.

"Reimei," she said. "Launch."

Calling her frame's new name, one half of the heroic duo dropped onto a battlefield teeming with monsters from another world.

One day, massive portals appeared all over the world. Later to be known as Gates, these were passages linking our world to another—a world filled with mankind's natural predators, the Jave. Ever since these Gates opened a few decades ago, Jave had been spilling through.

The Jave were fleshy beasts, purplish-black and shaped like cones or mantas. They had countless tentacles, each one several meters long. Humans caught by these tentacles were eaten whole.

The Jave made nests around the Gates, laid eggs, and multiplied on our world. The Imperial mainland was long since overrun with them; only a few survivors remained.

These survivors had settled on islands to the south, waging a desperate resistance against the Jave. These were the Jogen Islands, a crescent-shaped island chain stretching from the mainland of Japan across the ocean.

There were three major military encampments under Imperial Army control: one on Jogen, one floating on the waters near the Imperial Capital (which mankind had recovered only a month before), and one on a small island known as Aohime.

A new Gate had appeared above this last location, code-named Mid-Blue. This Gate obstructed the sea lane connecting the Capital and Jogen. If nothing was done, lines of supply and communication to the freshly recovered capital would remain unsecured, so the Imperial Army launched an operation to eliminate Mid-Blue.

In Mid-Blue airspace, sandwiched between the blue of the sky and the blue of the ocean, the horizon melted away, nearly

impossible to make out. Far in the distance was the volcanic island of Aohime. Just above that was the Gate, like a pitch-black moon surrounded by a red mist and a terrifying number of black specks.

The black specks were Jave, and the red mist was the blood they sprayed.

They were joined by white beams of light, outnumbering the black specks. These beams caused explosions, and the volume of red mist increased, but the number of black specks increased even more.

The war between the Imperial Air Force Mobile Unit and the Mid-Blue Jave swarm had begun.

The Air Force was deployed in a fan shape above Aohime Island. There were some aircraft and flying motherships, but the bulk of their forces were soldiers known as Maneuver Cavalleria. At a glance, they looked like skydivers, but that was not the case.

Each Cavalleria wore a frame of external armor. These frames were powered by the innate magical power all humans possessed, allowing them to fly. Known as Division Maneuvers, or DMs for short, the invention of these armored magic weapons had instantly made all weapons from the old world obsolete.

Cavalleria wearing sniper DMs began laying down cover fire from a distance. This was the storm of white beams seen a moment before. They carved through the Jave front lines, firing until their magic was almost tapped out. Nearly ten percent of the assembled black specks were eliminated.

"Attacker Squads, charge!"

At the commander's word, the snipers retreated, replaced by a crowd of Attacker units in two-man cells.

The Jave fought back. They fired bullets of light so fast they looked like twinkling stars. DMs were equipped with barriers known as Witch Bubbles that allowed them to move in the deep sea or outer space, but the monsters' shelling easily tore through these. Luck and reflexes allowed ninety percent of the attackers to make it through intact. That might sound like most, but it still meant dozens had perished.

The bulk of the DMs that the Air Force Cavalleria employed were ordinary Nichirin frames. Leaving the comm channels partially open, each frame was playing pre-selected combat music. Since this was proven to boost morale, the Air Force allowed DM units to play music as long as the volume was low enough that they wouldn't miss orders. The songs could be rock, punk, jazz, theme songs from mecha anime, or whatever the Cavalleria preferred, but they were almost all fast-paced and intense. The 2nd Mobile Unit's front attacker fired bullets in time to the rhythm of a double-bass drum set, the 10th Mobile Unit's attack gunner was shot down wrapped in the song of electronic fairies, and the 5th Mobile Unit's front attacker cut through an enemy Jave, screaming along with the chorus.

The odds were three to one in favor of the enemy.

Five seconds after the battle began, a tenth of the military's forces were gone, and the enemy numbers were only increasing.

How? Because a Queen had emerged from inside the Gate.

The Jave Queen was a massive cone-shaped monster three hundred meters in diameter. Made of red flesh, like internal organs, it had a horrifying number of mouths, and each of these spewed children—ordinary Jave. Their only shot at winning was to kill this Queen.

Six seconds had passed since the battle began.

The front lines had been disrupted, but the Jave swarm still held the skies over Aohime Island, and there were no signs of penetrating their inner stronghold.

But at the seven-second mark, a new frame fell from the skies above.

"Stay with me. Don't leave me alone. I will come back. Back to you."

Everyone heard these lyrics blasting over their comms. Whether through sheer nerve, or carelessness keeping her from noticing the volume was left cranked up, she was convinced no one else could hear—but if they listened close, they could hear her humming along. They pretended not to notice the barely suppressed note of fear.

A sweet song of love—not at all what you'd think the Warrior Princess would listen to.

Yet every one of them thought the same thing: *She's here. At last she's here. Right on time. Take it from here, Your Highness.*

An instant later, a blinding beam of light pierced the Queen Jave.

Screeeeeeeeeeeeeeeeeeeeeeeeeeeeeeeeeeeeeeeeeeeeeeeeeeeeee!

Shot by the Division Maneuver as it fell from 20,000 meters above, a third of the Queen's bulk was vaporized, and she screamed in pain and fury.

As if linked to her will, every Jave looked up just as a second shot fired. The horde of Jave were swallowed by the massive light bullet, vaporized one after another.

This beam was clearly far, far more powerful than anything the other Cavalleria had fired. The diameter alone was on a different scale. While an ordinary rifle fired fist-sized bursts of light, her bullets were so large that ten people could line up head to toe and still be swallowed up by them.

Her red DM fell, plunging through the hole she had made in the Jave swarm. The Jave all fired at her as she passed, but her DM danced across the surface of the ocean, dodging all their bullets. Several bullets appeared to score a direct hit, but a light like a black membrane appeared, catching and diverting them.

The shape of this DM was strange, not at all like a human's form. The head was too long, the wings too large, and the tail stretching from the back was too elongated. And the sheer size of it! It was at least twenty meters long.

Was it a bird? A crane? A dragon?

No...it was a Kiryu.

As the massive DM flew along the water's surface, several hexagon-shaped objects shot out ahead of it. They turned in the air, flying directly towards and into the Jave swarm where they exploded. The covers broke free, and countless guided light beams fired from within.

Numerous explosions followed. The Jave caught up in them were turned to dust.

Without checking the results, the giant DM was already

committed to its next action. As if kicking off the surface of the ocean, it suddenly rose upwards, hurling itself into the swarm. The Kiryu's head turned. Its mouth opened, and a beam of light shot out. Dozens of monsters died instantly.

This was the massive beam of light from earlier. The Kiryu's head turned left and right, mercilessly exterminating its foes. At the same time, the hexagons deployed from its tail—the guided light bullet containers—were fired into the thickest parts of the swarm, erupting and turning the walls of enemies into polka dots.

"Mother Servant Pod, fire."

At her whispered command, two dragons flew from her feet, splitting away from the main body. Those two dragons further split into dozens of birds, each flying like they had minds of their own, spewing light bullets from their tips. They were Type-2 Artillery Servants, sent into the midst of the enemy.

A storm of hundreds of light beams erupted, and the monsters from another world were incinerated one after another. The giant red DM passed through the enemy swarm again, climbing higher. Just before she was hidden by the sun, for a second, the other Cavalleria caught a glimpse of the pilot.

She was one of the Twin Star Heroes, a Division 5 named Suzuka Hanabi. She was from Jogen Maneuver Academy, High School Division, Class 3-A, Seat Number 12. Hanabi was an Attack Gunner from the Lunatic Order's Fuji Squad, wearing the frame called Reimei (Drag Ride).

She was also part of a giant dragon.

Drag Ride was the name of an advanced firepower unit made

exclusively for the Reimei frame. It was a mechanical dragon—a Kiryu—over ten times as tall as Hanabi herself. Hanabi was mounted on the underbelly of this beast like a kangaroo's joey, controlling it like her own arms and legs. Everything from the chest up was exposed, and she wielded a Scout Nova Rifle in both hands, but the lower portions of her body were entirely inside the Kiryu. Hanabi's head lay just below the dragon's long neck, and she wore a visor—generally not required with 6th generation DMs—allowing her to check the information provided by her new partner.

With the sun at her back, she did a flip, sending the Kiryu charging back into the thick of the Jave. The targets on her visor locked on to the Queen.

"High Nova Launcher..."

The primary cannon responded, the dragon's mouth yawning open.

"Fire!"

The cannon roared.

The ultra-wide beam cut a path through the enemy. The Queen reacted with a speed belying her bulk, avoiding a direct hit but still taking damage. The intense heat of the magic beam melted the flesh on the Queen's side, and she let out a scream that shook the very air, launching all her children at Hanabi. However, their feeble attacks were all blocked by the newly developed anti-light beam barrier, the Heavy Magic Field. This was the black membrane that briefly appeared around the DM after each hit. It was the Witch Bubble coated in a new tech called

Heavy Magic, and it effectively neutralized the Jave's bullets in a way never before possible. The clever Queen soon realized this, commanding her children to attack directly. *Props for judgment,* Hanabi thought.

A swarm of several hundred mantas flung themselves directly at Hanabi. She scattered guided light bullet containers like bait in her wake, launched dozens of Servants, and fired the rifle in her own hands, but it wasn't enough. Several mantas made it through the field, brushing against the Kiryu's wings.

"Ack!" Hanabi dropped the rifle, gathering Servants around both hands. Giant light swords stretched out from each of her palms, Blades made by merging several light beams. She then formed another twelve Servant Blades around herself, hacking away at any monsters who came near. Then...

Screeeeeeeeeeeeeeeeeeeeeeeeeeeeeeeeeeeeeeeeeeeeeeeeeeeeeee!

Light gathered in front of the injured Queen. She was charging a light shot, planning to shoot Hanabi and all the Jave gathered around her. Hanabi thought quickly. *Defense? Impossible. Even the Heavy Magic Field couldn't stand a hit of that size! Evasive maneuvers? Would they make it?*

The beam fired. An instant later...

Shichisei Kenbu: Shimetsu.

At the sound of the voice, the Queen's light bullet vanished with a *pop.*

Before Hanabi's eyes was the small back profile of a single Cavalleria, with nine bright wings fanned out around him. It was her partner's frame. He'd used a Shichisei Kenbu Machine

Fencing technique to quickly cover the ground and reach her in time. With the same motion as a karate left punch, he'd easily canceled out the fatal bullet.

Her partner was a front attacker with the Lunatic Order's Fuji Squad. Clad like a blue-armored warrior in a DM called the Soukyu (Pleiades), he was the other half of the Twin Star Heroes. Hanabi's own little hero, Okegawa Kuon.

"Kuon-kun!"

"Sorry, Senpai," he said, landing on Hanabi's—the Kiryu's—back.

"What are you doing? You aren't positioned here!" Hanabi yelled while moving at high speed, her Servant Blades slicing and dicing the swarming Jave.

Riding the Kiryu's back, Kuon pulled out two Ultra Magic Hardened Blades, turning Jave into sashimi as he replied, "That's why I said sorry."

"This again! You aren't sorry at all!"

"I am!"

They were always like this. But a new voice interrupted. "Hanabi-sama, lecturing him with that grin on your face isn't very convincing."

"Y-y-you shut up, En-kun!"

A fairy clad in what appeared to be a silk kimono altered to look like a uniform—the Guide AI known as En—made a point of appearing right before Hanabi's eyes just so she could smirk at her. "This is my master's love. Love!"

Hanabi went bright red. How could she bring that up now?!

"The plan was for me to draw the enemy away so you could finish off the Queen!" she yelled.

"Yep. Sorry! But..." Kuon detached himself from her back. The camera on the Kiryu's rear caught his face. He was smiling. "I'll go do that now, Senpai."

An instant later he was a blur, and then he was gone. En vanished with him.

Jeez. Hanabi turned over so the Kiryu's underside faced the Queen, giving herself a better view. The enemy had recovered from the shock of having her bullet canceled and was gathering light again when Kuon appeared behind it, using a *shukuchi* to cover the distance nigh-instantly.

Kuon took a deep breath, positioning himself on the Queen's back. As he examined his foe, he perceived within her the root of all life, the focal point of life energy—what his master called "the light of life". Almost leisurely, he thrust the Blade in his left hand towards it, releasing his breath.

Shichisei Kenbu Ultimate Art: Mumyo Tosen.

The Blade struck the Jave Queen in a nondescript section of flesh. But with the full force of Kuon's magic charging the Blade, it blew a wind of death through the fleshy monster, causing a phenomenon known as Magic Dispersal within it. This was the effect of Mumyo Tosen, a fatal art that forced all the magic within the enemy to self-destruct.

There was no resisting it.

Screeeeeeeeeeeeeeeeeeeeeeeeeeeeeeeeeeeeeeeeeeeeeeeeeee!!

A fourth scream echoed. The Queen's massive bulk slowly began to crumble, and the Gate over Aohime vanished, crackling like lightning. It had been a huge leap forward for the human race when they discovered that the Gates could only be maintained by a Jave Queen's magic.

It was obvious the lesser Jave had lost all coordination as they fell slowly through the air. Only the Queen's instructions had kept them focused; now, they were at a loss. The Kiryu and the rest of the mobile units attacked en masse, polishing off the survivors. The battle was as good as won.

"Is it over?" Kuon whispered.

"Yep. Well done, Kuon-sama," his Guide AI said, appearing before him and bowing. "An art with a one hundred percent chance of causing death! I've seen it before, but...that's so broken!"

"Broken how?" His Guide sometimes said things he didn't understand.

"But if you push yourself too..."

"I'm fine."

"If you say so...but Kuon-sama, since the plan was for a sneak attack, they removed all the extra boosters."

"Yep."

"All your nozzles are going, yet your falling speed seems unaffected."

"Well, this frame was never designed to fly."

"That ocean's coming up fast."

"It is."

"You may have a Witch Bubble protecting you, but if you hit it at this speed, it's definitely gonna hurt!"

"Oh, dear." He considered trying to soften it with a shukuchi, but...

"What *are* you doing?"

"Hm?"

A dragon flew in from the side, catching him in its mouth before flying off. The dragon's head bent, holding him where the pilot could see. His gallant and adorable Cavalleria was very obviously forcing her grin into a stern expression. "Hanabi-senpai, thank you," he said.

"Thank you, Kuon-kun. No, wait..."

There were no enemies left on the radar. They'd been wiped out. Kuon looked the dragon over. "Seems like you're handling the Drag Ride well."

"Don't change the subject!"

Darn.

"...You've been getting awfully bold lately, Kuon-kun."

"Have I?"

"You have! Remember to respect your elders!"

"I thought I was."

As they bickered, shouts of victory were raised around them. While the Cavalleria celebrated, orders to return to the mother-ship were handed down, one after another. There were many voices praising the heroes, but Hanabi seemed oblivious to them. "I...I know that, but..." The dragon's head turned, bringing Kuon even closer. He noticed that Hanabi's face was extraordinarily

beautiful, pretty, cute...and a little flushed. "You can let me baby you a little!"

Oh, he thought. *She's in Maiden Mode.*

"The other day we had that d-d-d-d-date... I mean, shopping trip, and you... All your money..."

Uh-oh. "Err, Hanabi-senpai?"

"Wh-what? You repent?"

"Um...you know your comms are wide open, right?"

"Huh?"

The shouts of victory gave way to whistles, laughter, and teasing. "Good job, Princess! Found you a good one, huh?" "Such passion! Talk about covering yourself with glory!" "Whoa, phrasing!"

"What?!" Hanabi had frozen up completely. Kuon put his hands to his head. This wasn't going well. He wracked his brains looking for a way to save her, or at least share the pain of this shame. He couldn't let her be the only one embarrassed. He wanted to share the burden. The world no longer needed solo heroes, after all. The two of them were a team.

"Senpai, uh..." He was pretty sure this was the manliest thing he'd ever done. "I love you!"

The Warrior Princess turned redder than her own frame, let out a really adorable squeal, and dropped Kuon into the ocean.

The next day, the entire Air Force was talking about Suzuka Hanabi.

On the bridge of the *Kuou*, a girl was watching the fight on screen.

"What do you think, Nürburg-kun? How's the Drag Ride moving?"

"Not bad." the girl—Nürburg—responded mechanically.

"Good," the captain nodded.

She looked at the screen again, at the other hero on it. "That's my brother," she whispered so quietly that no one else heard it.

DIVISIONMANEUVER

CHAPTER 7

The Hero Investigated

ONCE, THERE WAS a Hero named Suzuka Hachishiki. He was a Maneuver Cavalleria, Captain of the Imperial Air Force City Defense Corps 1st Mobile Unit, Suzuka Squad...a man who'd killed, slaughtered, and massacred monsters from another world.

His parents, the nuns and his friends at the orphanage who had taken him in, and the comrades he'd made in the army after enlisting had all been killed by Jave. But Hachishiki survived one reckless assault after another, fueled both by a desire for revenge and the urge to follow his fallen friends into death. As a result, he saved countless lives and found himself celebrated as the Hero.

Thirteen years ago, he died in battle against an enemy Queen.

However, just before he died, a side effect of the Gate sent his soul into the body of a newborn. The Hero was reborn with all his memories intact. His magic, however...not so much.

Magic was required to pilot a Division Maneuver. Magic was rated on a scale of one to five. He'd been a Division 5, the strongest mankind was capable of, but now he was bumped all the way down to Division 1.

The former Hero, now reborn as Okegawa Kuon, faced this fact at the tender age of five, a fate so cruel it made him cry. It had sent him into a total meltdown.

But he didn't give up.

Reunited with Nanahoshi Kaede, his master in his previous life, he dedicated himself anew to the study of Shichisei Kenbu Machine Fencing. He made that impressive strength his own, entered Jogen Maneuver Academy despite his division, and met the strongest student the school had ever had—a Division 5 named Suzuka Hanabi. He joined her team, they made each other better, and their hearts grew as one.

Tasked with closing the Gate over the Capital, Hanabi and the rest of the team had been in mortal danger, but Kuon arrived in time, rescued Hanabi from the enemy's clutches, killed the Queen, and destroyed the Gate.

Suzuka Hanabi's efforts allowed many Cavalleria to retreat from the battlefield.

Okegawa Kuon's efforts saved Hanabi's team and destroyed both the Queen and the Gate.

In return for their achievements, the Air Force gave the duo a new name: The Twin Star Heroes.

Additionally, Kuon discovered that the senpai he loved was a girl he'd saved in his previous life. However, Suzuka Hanabi did not yet know that the boy she loved was the reincarnation of the Hero who'd saved her, whom she'd looked up to her entire life.

That was a close one.

Okegawa Kuon let out a sigh of relief. Broadcasting their flirting to the entire Air Force during an operation was unprecedented. If his master hadn't pulled some strings, even the Twin Star Heroes could both have been thrown in solitary.

Instead, they'd been let off with a three-page essay and three hundred push-ups each. They might be called heroes, but both Kuon and Hanabi were still trainees.

Right now, they were in a room at Jogen Maneuver Academy. "I'm sorry, Kuon-kun..."

"D-don't worry about it, Senpai."

They'd both managed to get their essays done and then started doing push-ups together in the headmaster's office. Hanabi had made it to two hundred and then found herself unable to move, so Kuon took over her extra hundred. After all, they were a team. "My body's lighter, so it's less work," Kuon said, trying to make her feel better. This backfired.

"Oh? You don't say?" Nanahoshi Kaede said, sitting down on his back mid-push-up. She was his master and the one who'd ostensibly saved them. As Hanabi watched ruefully, cursing her unresponsive arm muscles, Kuon kept counting, "Two hundred sixteen, two hundred seventeen!" He voiced no complaints about his extra burden, but there was quite a puddle of sweat forming under him. Keeping up a good rhythm was vital in these situations. He just had 184 to go. He could do it.

"Hanabi?" Kaede asked. "You look like you want to say something."

"I absolutely don't!"

"Your slices got dull as that last fight went on, didn't they? Even with a DM on, if you don't visualize the movements clearly, your body won't keep up. You've got a mental limit telling you that you can only swing a sword for so long. And you know why that is?"

"...Because that's how long I can swing a sword without the DM."

"Exactly. So you understand the reason for this punishment? Then why have you stopped?"

"Ungggh..."

"The reason your biceps gave out is because of your excessive chest blubber." Kaede poked Hanabi's boobs with her wooden sword. It was midsummer, and the school trainee uniforms were quite thin. Hanabi's massive boobs swung all over the place. It was mesmerizing. Kaede's behavior was verging on sexual harassment, and in another military school there might be consequences, but at Jogen Maneuver Academy, you were better off saying "yes" to whatever the headmaster came up with.

Thus Hanabi was forced to yell, "You're completely correct, ma'am!"

Meanwhile, Kuon was entering his 218th arm extension, thinking, *Pot calling the kettle black, you big-boobed loli cougar.*

"Kuooon? I feel like I should be giving you can extra fifty just because..."

Dang, she always knows. She never misses a beat.

"Two hundred nineteeeeen!" he roared.

He only had 231 more. He could do it.

As she bullied her pupils, Kaede shook her head.

Cards on the table—she was the one who'd hacked Hanabi's frame and opened up her comms. She'd figured if Kuon and Hanabi started talking, odds were good they'd get flirty. If they'd kept their private lives out of the mission, she'd never have been able to administer this punishment, but...well, that hadn't happened.

She had a legitimate reason for doing this.

The military brass were hell-bent on covering Hanabi in glory, treating her like an idol, their very own Joan of Arc. But Kaede had seen what that treatment had done to her former student, Suzuka Hachishiki, and she was not about to lose anyone else the way she had him.

Thanks to Kuon's stupidity, everyone now knew the Twin Star Heroes were partners on and off the battlefield, and that would protect Hanabi from the worst kinds of idol worship. Being the Warrior Princess was plenty.

They no longer needed a single Hero, but venerating a duo instead made little difference. The result would still be the two of them being used and getting killed.

"We don't need a Hero who stands above us all."

Words she'd said herself five and a half months earlier, but the reality wasn't quite so easy.

"I really am sorry, Kuon-kun..."

As the headmaster's door closed, Hanabi was in full Maiden Mode, her shoulders drooping. "It's my fault we got punished, but you ended up taking on my share..."

"It's fine, Senpai. I'm used to it!" Kuon tried thumping his chest but couldn't raise his arms.

The number of Gates over the Imperial mainland remained in double digits. Some were no longer active, while some were still going strong. It would be bad if they didn't close them fast, but lack of resources meant they were forced to ignore them.

Three days had passed since they'd eliminated the Gate over Aohime Island. Hanabi spent those days at weapons development organizing new weapon data and adjusting her frame, and this was the first appearance she'd put in at school. Kuon himself had been busy with his own military duties, so even though they were a couple and attended the same school, being summoned to the headmaster's office was the first time they'd seen each other since that fight. Such were the times they lived in, but still...

Perhaps having a girlfriend for the first time in thirty years (counting both his lives together) had robbed Kuon of his mental tranquility. Suzuka Hachishiki had built armor around his heart out of hatred for the Jave and a desire for revenge, but now that armor had been pried away, exposing the weaknesses within and leaving him unstable. It came as a shock to find he was feeling lonely. Even realizing this fact came as a blow.

After the battle for the Capital, they'd returned to school, and on one occasion the two of them had gone shopping together, but that was as close to a date as they'd managed. This was also partially because they'd both become rather famous. Everywhere they went, people recognized them and caused a commotion. Their date only lasted two hours.

Kuon wanted the two of them to at least spend some time together today. With that thought in mind, he began, "Um, Hanabi-senp—"

"Okegawa-sensei! We've come to meet you!!" A number of burly men ran up to him, all wearing Air Force uniforms.

"Oh...thanks..." Kuon said listlessly.

The men weren't just soldiers with the Air Force but also Kuon's students. Okegawa Kuon had been ordered to serve as the Air Force Machine Fencing instructor. Men two or three times his age were calling him "Okegawa-sensei" or "assistant instructor". Understandably, a group opposed to the idea of a thirteen-year-old teacher had proposed a mock battle, and as a result, he'd cut through scores of veteran Cavalleria. Since they were all close-quarter battles, he hadn't even used Nine-Count Strike. Okegawa Kuon had proven beyond all doubt that he was the Air Force's best swordsman.

"Oh, is that Suzuka Hanabi-dono with you?"

"The legendary Bushi Hime! Your beauty is even greater than they say. You're the jewel of the Air Force!"

Such obvious platitudes. Coming to meet me was clearly just an excuse to see her in the flesh, Kuon thought.

Hanabi activated Warrior Mode and put her hand on her chest, saluting the Cavalleria. "Well met, Air Force Senpai. I hear you've been very helpful to my partner."

"Not at all—he's the one helping us!"

"Sorry to snatch him away from you."

Everyone sounded perfectly polite, but they were clearly letting this get to their heads.

Kuon was just a little bit put out. He stepped in front of Hanabi, pointing to the exit. "Men! Go on ahead! I'll be right behind."

"Yes, sir!" They saluted, grinning. They were perhaps all too aware of their young instructor's fit of jealousy. They'd all survived their share of rough situations and had plenty of life experience.

Kuon sighed and turned back to Hanabi. "Sorry, Hanabi-senpai. I've got to get back to my duties."

"Yes... I'm still working on adjustments to the Kiryu. I suppose this is goodbye."

"Also, sorry about my students. I told them not to come gawk at you, but..."

"I don't mind. Getting treated like a hero with you isn't the worst thing. Although I think only you really deserve the honor. You're the Cavalleria who deserves to follow in Suzuka Hachishiki's footsteps."

"Er, no—"

"But that doesn't mean I'm giving up! I want to be a hero just as much as you do."

The smile Hanabi gave him caused a sizzling pain in Kuon's heart. She didn't seem to be aware of it, but whenever Hanabi

talked about Suzuka Hachishiki, a look of intense pride and joy swept over her. She really admired him. Her goal was to be like the man who'd saved her life.

Kuon hadn't told Hanabi that he'd been her hero in his previous life. His master had forbidden it. But even if she hadn't...

That look on her face... I really can't tell her.

He'd changed so much. He wasn't her hero anymore. He was just a cocky little kid five years younger than her, demoted from a Division 5 to a Division 1. He was scared that it would shatter her image of him if he told her. More than anything, he was scared she wouldn't love him anymore.

So he couldn't tell her.

He felt guilty about it, but he didn't think he had a choice.

_//////////⌐

Meanwhile, a German exchange student was arriving at the Jogen Maneuver Academy. She was in the Exchange Program for Mobile Maneuver and Heavy Magic Research. There were many people surprised that Germany still existed, but it would be more accurate to say that it had returned from the dead.

Forty years ago, a Gate appeared over Nürburg Castle (as did Gates all across Europe), spewing countless Jave that ran roughshod over Western Europe. But one day, thirty years ago, they stopped completely. The Gate ceased to function.

To the naked eye, the Gate remained unchanged—a wide black hole creepily hovering over Nürburg. But for thirty years,

not one Jave emerged. In those thirty years, Germany and the countries around it fought back. All of the Jave which had emerged from the Gate, as well as the Jave born on this side of it, were eliminated by the Mobile Maneuver Corps. It was a massive, fantastic victory.

Several hundred years before the invention of Division Maneuvers had been the Great Disaster of the previous era. The very same people who overcame that threat to mankind now preserved their culture via the Division Maneuvers.

However, the Gate remained.

All who looked up at the sky wondered the same thing: *How can we rid ourselves of that black moon?* They'd driven the monsters out, and Europe was at peace, but the people looking up at the sky also thought: *Is it really?*

Enemies had suddenly stopped pouring out of the Gate, and they'd polished off all the ones that remained, but did that really mean they were rid of them?

According to the account of the German Air Force's military actions, after the Gate appeared over Nürburg Castle, the Germans repeatedly retreated, withdrawing their front lines. Eventually, they were forced to make the tough call to abandon their country altogether. The next day, the Gate abruptly ceased all activity. Putting aside the differences of the previous era, the Mobile Maneuver Corps of each Western European country banded together, and there was a period of intense fighting until the territories of man were recovered.

Weirdly, nowhere in the records were the words "massive,"

"mothership," "boss," or "Queen" mentioned. The words "Rochen" and "Oktopus" appeared countless times, alongside words for devils or monsters, but the word "Königin"? Not once.

They didn't know.

The tens of thousands of monsters slaughtered in Europe were all weak monsters sent by a Jave Queen as a test to see if they could survive on the other side. In other words, these monsters were more intelligent than the famous fictional aliens who came all the way from Mars only to be killed by the common cold.

The Germans had just realized this fact six months ago.

It was a few days after Mid-Blue had been eliminated. After school let out at the Jogen Maneuver Academy, the Fuji Squad was gathered in their meeting room. Without warning, the door opened, and a girl stepped in the room.

"*Guten tag.*"

She had pale skin and black hair in a bob. Her eyes were brown, and she looked very young—ten years old at most. She wore a dress with some goth-loli touches, but something about her still looked like an old Japanese doll. She was clearly Japanese, yet something about her seemed very much *not*.

"*Guten tag,*" she said again, expressionless. Her eyes were wide open but unmoving. The phrase "eyes like ice" did not quite seem to suffice. Ice melted. It moved. This girl didn't. Her gaze locked on nothing, just stared fixedly at empty space. It was as if she'd just stopped there, unmoving, utterly without any facial expression.

Like a thing.

Like a machine.

Like a doll.

This level of expressionlessness was downright astonishing. In fact, neither the squad leader, Fuji Jindo, nor the sniper, Motegi Rin, managed to respond at all.

Only Hanabi, in Warrior Mode, managed to splutter, "U-uh, so you're the one the headmaster managed—"

The girl's head turned—only her head. Like a doll. *"Guten tag,"* she repeated a third time.

Hanabi let out a little squeak, overwhelmed, and managed nothing further. It was much too creepy.

Kuon was forced to take over just by process of elimination. "Um...you're the exchange student from Germany... Tooka-chan, was it?" Their ages weren't all that different, but he was going with -chan anyway.

Once again, only her head turned, her eyes staring blankly at him, but Kuon had seen it before and was ready for it. He braced himself like he was preparing to enter combat.

"Onii-chan..." Tooka went still again. Without her expression wavering one iota, she said, "Are you my brother?"

A tear rolled down her cheek without warning.

"Er? What? Sorry, huh?"

Kuon was thoroughly rattled now. Of course he was. A total stranger had just called him her brother and started to cry. But the real surprise was yet to come.

"Onii-chan...!" Tears streaming down her cheeks, Tooka threw her arms around Kuon. She might have been about three years younger than him, but their heights were very similar. Her teary face was right next to his, her little chin rested on his shoulder. Her hands were clasped behind his back, hugging him very tightly.

"Whaaaaaaat...?!" Kuon froze up, question marks pouring out of him. His eyes were locked on Fuji, who looked like a pigeon shot by a satellite cannon, and Rin, who'd recovered first and was aiming her Device camera at him.

Hanabi, on the other hand, looked like a market crash had just wiped out all her stocks. Her expression had drained so thoroughly that Kuon instantly started formulating his defense. *This isn't...!*

The cause of this horror finally detached herself from him, saying, "I finally found you, onii-chan." She didn't seem particularly happy about this, but then she kissed him tenderly on the cheek. "Now we can be together forever," she whispered.

Her voice seemed so very far away.

"Do you believe in past lives?" she whispered.

This seemed extremely sketchy.

"We were brother and sister in a past life."

"P-past life...?" His heart skipped a beat. Anyone else would have laughed this off but not Kuon. After all, he had clear memories of his own previous life, when he'd been...

"Yes, in my previous life I was Akigase Tooka. And you were Suzu—"

She was cut off by a loud noise. Everyone turned, startled.

"Yeah, that's what I thought would happen," Kaede said, looking annoyed. She'd slammed the door open and was glaring at Tooka. "Didn't I tell you not to bring that up yet?"

"Right. Sorry, Mother," Tooka said, bowing her head.

Kaede sighed and turned to the Fuji Squad. "Let me introduce you. This is my other student, Tooka Nürburg. She'll be representing the Drag Ride developers and serving as the team mechanic. Try to get along."

There was a brief silence, and then Fuji and Rin glanced at each other, muttering...

"Drag Ride developer?"

"The headmaster's student?"

Kaede rephrased. "She made Hanabi's new frame, and she's a Shichisei Kenbu student—Kuon's 'sister' in that sense."

Either of those things alone would be impressive. All eyes focused on Tooka, who was still clinging to Kuon. She finally let him go, turned towards the others, and spoke with her expression completely unchanging. "Nice to meet you," she said, her voice clear as a bell. She bowed, a clean, robotic movement.

"You're sunk, Hanabi," Rin whispered.

Hanabi had yet to move a muscle.

Tooka Nürburg.
Estimated age: Ten.

Profession: Division Maneuver Developer/Mechanic/etc.

Division 5.

Parents: Unknown.

Actual Age: Unknown.

Birthplace: Unknown.

Memories Prior to the Age of Five: Lost.

She was a mystery.

Five years ago, a girl had been found lying under the Gate at Germany's Nürburg Castle by the international alliance and German military. Situational evidence suggested she was a civilian who'd gotten caught up in the battle to recover Nürburg... except that was impossible, because that territory was controlled by Jave until the armed forces arrived. The best explanation anyone could come up with was that she was a civilian who came back through the Gate—the first person ever to do so.

When she woke up, she was found to have no memories of her first five years of life. All she remembered was the name "Tooka", and that she was the heir to the Shichisei Kenbu arts. Kaede was summoned to Germany but had no memories of Tooka. And yet the child was so clearly fond of her that she ended up accepting her as a student. Based on how Kaede had accepted strange orphans like Hachishiki, Kuon, and Tooka as students, children were clearly her weakness.

Tooka was sent to school in Germany, where her talents blossomed. She discovered one new DM theory after another, developed them, and earned her doctorate. All the researchers in

her field said the same thing: she discovered things like she knew them all along.

Where was she from?

Who was she?

She remained a mystery, but one thing was perfectly clear: this genius ten-year-old Maneuver developer *loved* sweets. Her favorite involved mixing flour, water, sugar, butter, and eggs, and dipping the dough in hot oil and then sprinkling more sugar on top.

"You like it?"

"Yes."

"We have more. Eat all you like."

"Thank you." She was currently seated next to Fuji, inhaling a donut. A round sugar donut. Sweet, fluffy, and dangerous. On the video desk were three Mistel Donut boxes and as many coffee cups as there were people. The sweet scent filled the meeting room.

On the other side of the desk, Rin was gnawing on an Old Fashioned, giving Hanabi her honest opinion. "All that talk about past lives... Is she all right in the head?"

Hanabi took a bite out of a Pon de Ring. She was saving a Double Chocolate and a Chocolate Old Fashioned for Kuon. "Manners, Rin. She's the headmaster's student and the chief mechanic for the Kiryu."

"So why's she calling Kyuu-kun 'onii-chan?'"

"Students of the same martial arts school are all siblings."

"In such an emotional way? Gimme that chocolate one."

"They'd never met before, it was a touching moment. And no! Those are for Kuon-kun."

"Tch. Tell me, Hanabi, when you first met Kyuu-kun, did you react like that?"

"Not quite. My mind went totally blank, and there was a pain in my chest that—I mean, none of your business!"

"You were weirdly in sync during that mock battle. Reimei's a ranged frame, and yet you went in for a close-range fight."

"L-L-L-Leave me out of this!"

Rin finished her donut and took a sip of her iced café au lait. Reaching for a French Cruller, she said, "She calls herself a student, but it doesn't sound like she's learned *any* Machine Fencing."

"Well, she's a Division 5, like me. The headmaster has no intention of teaching her anything. But she insisted she had to be a student."

"Maybe she looks up to the Hero like you do."

"Mm."

"Like you, she survived a war zone when she was very little."

"Mm."

"So you're the same! Go talk to her. Don't be scared!"

"I-I'm not, but...eep!"

Rin gave her a shove, and Hanabi was forced to either stand or fall off her chair. The box with the chocolate donuts survived intact.

"Hm? What is it, Suzuka-kun?" Fuji said, confused.

"E-er...well..."

Tooka was just staring at her. It was impossible for Hanabi

to tell what she was thinking. The hand holding the box started sweating. She scratched it and took a deep breath. *I can do this.* "N-Nürburg-ku—"

Before she could even finish the name, the girl looked up at her and said, "Tooka is fine."

Already feeling like the rug had been pulled out from under her, Hanabi managed to retain her footing. "T-Tooka-kun."

"Yes, Hanabi-oneesama?"

"...Onee-sama?"

"Mother...Master informed me that Kiryu's official rider is also onii-chan's lover. Which would make you my sister."

"I-It does...?"

"It does," Tooka intoned flatly, her voice betraying no emotion at all.

Hanabi felt like she was talking to an alarm clock. En was an AI, and even she was way more human than Tooka.

The alarm clock bowed her head. "Thank you for taking such good care of my brother. Whatever his flaws, I hope you will continue to help him out."

"Er, uh...sure..."

She had a sister-in-law? Why did that feel like defeat?

The alarm clock bowed her head again. "There's a flaw when turning."

"Huh?"

"The Kiryu."

"O-oh, right. When I roll left, there's just a sliiight sluggishness...like interference in the relays or Servant connectivity."

It was pure happenstance that she'd managed to catch and follow this sudden change of subject.

"Understood. I will look into it and should have adjustments made in the morning."

"That soon? Our engineers have been looking for a week without finding the root cause."

"Kiryu is my child." Tooka did not smile.

"I-I see...well, you certainly are on the ball for your age...like..." Hanabi looked over at Kuon, who was deep in a serious-looking discussion with Kaede at the back of the room.

Hanabi thought Kuon and Tooka definitely had something in common. They were similar in some ways.

"What is it?" Tooka asked, head to one side.

Hanabi waved her hands to say it was nothing and then held one out. "Nice to meet you, anyway. I'm Suzuka Hanabi. Thanks for taking care of Kiryu for me."

Her new chief mechanic, and Kuon's sister student, shook her hand, expressionless. "Tooka Nürburg. Nice to meet you, too."

That was how the strange relationship between the two girls closest to Kuon began.

When Kuon finished talking to Kaede, Hanabi said, "I saved the chocolate ones for you," and he looked really happy. Her feelings of defeat lessened.

But only a little.

That evening, in a room in the Jogen Maneuver Academy Girls' Dormitory...

A digital window had been opened above a pillow, the screen scrolling through Jogen Island event information. Nearly all the fields were blank.

"Hmm..."

Motegi Rin was lying face-down on her dorm bed, idly scanning this information page, when she heard footsteps outside the door. Then the noise of the electronic lock disengaging. That alone was enough to tell her who was coming in.

She glanced at the clock. 9:17 PM. *Well past the dorm curfew, but she'd almost certainly cleared it with the dorm mother and had been let in through the back door,* Rin thought. She closed her window. "Welcome back, Hanabi."

"Mm, thanks."

Rin turned her head to see Suzuka Hanabi in uniform—honestly, it never looked right on her, like she was a little too beautiful for it—as she walked to her bed, slippers shuffling, and put her bag down.

Hanabi was Rin's childhood friend, stepsister, squad mate, classmate, and roommate. She was cute as she was gallant. Rin noticed circles under Hanabi's eyes as she collapsed straight onto her bed with a thump. Hanabi burrowed under her covers. "They're really wearing you out, huh?" Rin asked.

"...Mmph."

A muffled groan was the only response. Rin took that as a yes. "You gonna take a shower?"

"Unh."

It was rare to see Hanabi like this. Normally, no matter how tired she got, she would at least wash her hands and face, and take a shower before resting. Rin knew the answer but asked anyway. "Something happen?"

"Mrgh."

"Not the new weapon, right?"

Hanabi didn't answer. She was shutting her out.

Rin's Device rang with an unfamiliar ringtone. She popped a window open and answered. "Hello? Dorm Mother? ...What? A visitor at the door? Kyuu-kun?"

Hanabi bolted upright in instant panic. Her eyes darted left and right, back and forth, and then finally found the window and looked down at the entrance. She stared into the darkness, searching.

There was nobody there.

Rin sighed. "I'm kidding, Hanabi."

Hanabi spun around, her face astonishingly red. "Y-you're... you...!! You're just...!!"

Rin closed the empty window, set her ringtone back to normal, and waved Hanabi to a seat. Then she stood up, opened the door, and stuck her head out to make sure no one was there. The room to the right was empty, and Nao and Sachikou from the room on the left were playing mahjong in the lobby with the Amakusa sisters. There was an analog game fad going on in the Jogen girls' dorm, in its third year running with no signs of dying down. Manual stalking, no Devices, arinashi rules. She'd have to ask tomorrow which method of cheating had led to more wins.

"All clear," Rin said.

"Rin...?" Hanabi asked, confused.

Rin winked at her and then joined Hanabi on her bed, lying next to her. She locked arms with her and pulled her in close. *Man, she really smells good. Even though she hasn't showered!* Rin thought. *All right, close quarters combat engaged, right to the Core.* "What happened with Kyuu-kun?"

Hanabi made a little noise.

Yep, he was definitely behind this. Jeez. "You have a fight?"

"Not a fight..."

"Then what?"

"Just...nothing."

"What do you mean?"

"We just haven't...done anything. Anything at all. Nothing...!" Hanabi buried her face in her hands. "It's been a month since we recovered the Capital, but we've only been on one d-d-d...shopping trip!"

Don't give up.

"A date, you mean."

"W-we haven't done those and we've barely even seen each other and definitely not talked at all and...today I thought we were finally going to get some time together, but we were pulled apart immediately...and I could only manage two hundred push-ups and I want to have Kuon teach me Fencing, too!"

Rin thought two hundred push-ups was an impressive number for any girl.

"And then that transfer student Tooka-kun gave him a hug and...!"

Oh yeah, that was great. He looked like he'd been caught cheating. Too funny.

"And I just thought, are we not actually going out at all? Are we even together? M-maybe I just think we are, and Kuon-kun doesn't even know it. Maybe he'd prefer someone closer to his age, like Tooka-kun. Wh-what do you think, Rin?"

With a herculean effort, Rin managed to frown. She was on the verge of laughing out loud, otherwise. It had been a long time since she'd had so much trouble suppressing a laugh. *Right. So that explains it.* "Ha...d-don't worry, Hanabi," she snorted.

"Why do you look like you're trying not to laugh?"

"...Ahem. No, it's nothing. Mm. Right...don't worry, Hanabi. Kyuu-kun is crazy about you."

"H-he is...?" Hanabi's smile was super embarrassed but really happy.

Gosh, she's adorable. "You heard him, didn't you? He said he loved you with his comms wide open so the whole Air Force could hear him."

"Aughhhhhhhhh!!" At the very mention of comms, Hanabi hid her face in her pillow and started thrashing her limbs around.

"Ask anybody. They'll tell you Kyuu-kun is crazy for Hanabi. Although you might hear some concerns about you going for a kid that young..."

"Kmph-kmp ismph a kmph!" Hanabi exclaimed, her voice muffled by the pillow.

Rin chuckled. *I think she said "Kuon-kun isn't a kid!" Probably.* "He does seem more like an old fart."

Hanabi managed to pull her face out of the pillow to argue. "Th-that's what's good about him! The way he always acts so mature but occasionally does something super childish is so cute and cool, and he's little but always comes through and..."

"I know, I know, you adore him, I get it."

"Arghh...!" Rin was forced to restrain her. "But..." Hanabi whispered, shoulders slumping again. "...does he really?"

Wow, her mood is all over the place, Rin thought. "Forget how you get no time together, forget this new rival-slash-little sister—is anything else bothering you?"

"Well...well...Kuon-kun...he...he won't..."

"Won't what?"

"He never..."

"Never what?"

"Calls me by my name!"

This was too much for Rin. She threw open the window, screaming, "Maideeeeeeeeeeeeeeeeeeen!"

From somewhere in the distance, someone else yelled back, "Shut up, Motegi!" *Oops.*

"It's just a naaame! I mean, he calls me 'Rin-san!' I don't even rate a 'Senpai!'"

"Mm, yeah, well, you aren't really the senpai type, Rin..."

"You wound me!" Rin flopped back down on the bed.

"On our...our date," Hanabi continued. "We didn't even hold hands...or...k-k-kiss...even though before we went into combat we... Oh, I'm getting embarrassed just thinking about it!"

"Wait...back up, Hanabi." When she heard Hanabi's wail, an

image came to Rin's mind: a door made of darkness with a sign on it, warning her not to step farther in. She hesitated a second and then kicked the sign in two. "Tell me more."

"Like I said, before we were deployed..." The rest was whispered.

"Whaaaat?! You not only kissed, you whaaaaaaat?! *Whaaaaat?!*"

The window was flung open once more.

"She beat me to iiiiiiiiiiiiiiiiiiiit!"

Multiple voices shot back. "For Christ's sake, Motegi!"

Sorry, sorry. She shut the window and turned back around to find Hanabi surprised.

"Er, uh, wait, you haven't yet?"

"Wow, do you even know how smug that sounds?"

"I-I mean, you didn't come home that evening and...you're so popular and...it was the night before we got deployed, so I thought you were with someone yourself..."

Rin couldn't admit she'd been tailing them. Instead, she clenched a fist. "Damn you, Kyuu-kun! Violating my Hanabi...! I'm gonna stick you in the fryer!"

"V-violate...?! Oh!"

Don't turn red now! "Hmm, well, okay, don't worry. Motegi Rin has your back!"

"No, I'd prefer you stay out of it..."

Rin pretended not to hear that. She wasn't letting something this fun pass unmeddled with! She instantly pulled up their squad leader on her Device.

He answered alarmingly fast, before the second ring. "What's up, Motegi-kun? Emergency?"

"Totally. Never been anything more urgent."

"In that case, I can assume there's no rush at all. But I suppose I'll hear you out..."

"Practice next week. Wednesday."

"You have a proposal?"

"Hanabi will be with us that day, right?"

"Suzuka-kun?"

"Yes, she's in a state. And we need to throw Tooka-chan a welcome party, so...blah blah."

"...Hmm?"

"Blah blah."

"...Hmm?"

"Blah-blah-blah. Blah."

"...You're a real piece of work. Still...sure, fine."

"Nice, Squad Leader! You're a man who gets it!"

"For the sake of the team. And if Suzuka-kun and Okegawa-kun are in a state like that, I'm not about to ignore it. I'll do what I can."

"Ha! The taken man knows what's up! Cool!"

Fuji started to protest this, but Rin just hung up on him. She spun around. "Mwa ha ha! Hanabi...just you wait."

"Um, Rin...what are you plotting...?"

All she had to do was wink at her, and Hanabi would relax. But instead, Rin just maintained a malicious smirk.

The next day, on the practice grounds...

Kuon lay flat on his back.

"You've got a lot to work on." Headmaster Kaede said.

"Yeah." Practicing with his Master for the first time in a while, he suspected he might be getting punished for using the ultimate art during the Mid-Blue battle. Punishment or no, he was getting thrashed.

He had a wooden sword. She was unarmed. Yet no matter what angle he approached from, he ended up being sent flying. *It doesn't make sense,* Kuon thought. *I'm better at Fencing than I was in my previous life, but...*

He heard her voice from above. "You've been training for nineteen years, right?"

"This is my twentieth."

She nodded. "Good a number as any. Spend the next twenty years learning to Fence without a sword."

"What does that even mean?"

"It means if you're relying on your weapon, you've got a long way to go."

But..."Fencing" implies the use of swords. "But you've taught me the ultimate move," he protested.

"And something that risky shouldn't be used willy-nilly. That's also just the surface!"

"Surface...?"

"Shichisei Kenbu has depth! The Eight Hidden Forms you're about to start learning include arts that can only be learned with the right type of magic."

"So...these'll be as hard as a Division 1?"

"Not necessarily. It isn't the amount of magic but the characteristics of it. I'm a Division 4, but I was only the right fit for four of them. Okegawa Kuon...over the next twenty years, you should aim to surpass me."

"Master...how old are you, rea—guh!"

She stomped on him.

In the car on the way home, his master broke her sullen silence to ask, "What's up with Hanabi? You two doing well?"

Lately Kaede had started driving Kuon home after practice. Kuon liked her aircar; it was a little white round retro number. Despite its size, she'd somehow stuck a pre-electric V8 engine in the thing, and the unexpected power was so her. The lack of interior space was a small price to pay.

Kuon realized that he'd actually known Nanahoshi Kaede longer than his own mother.

That was all the more reason why this sudden personal question raised his hackles. He and his Master had never once talked about his personal life before, and she never even mentioned his relationship with Hanabi until now. He chose his words carefully. "Um...yes. We get along..."

"No problems?"

"Not *none*, but..."

"Oh? What's the problem? Spit it out."

"Well..." Watching his Master's face carefully, Kuon admitted they hadn't seen much of each other.

Kaede kept her eyes on the road. Safe driving was a priority. "Hmm. I see. You've got a team meeting Wednesday?"

"Um, where'd you hear—"

"I'll drop you off. It's a remote location; hard to get to without a car."

"Uh, thanks..."

"Don't be late." She nodded, but there was a worried look in her eyes.

_//////////⌐

That Wednesday evening, as dusk began descending...

On the outskirts of town was a large mountain, upon which was perched a mansion seemingly larger than their school. It had a massive front gate. Everything about it screamed "military stronghold"...or possibly "yakuza lair." It was the home of the Motegi family, the most powerful on the Jogen Islands.

A ridiculously beautiful girl stood outside the entrance. Wearing a pink yukata, her long black hair tied up, she kept touching the back of her head, as if this whole look was embarrassing her. Her chest had been forced into the yukata somehow, but it definitely called attention to itself, and the curve of her backside was also all too prominent.

"Nnnnghh..."

She was, of course, Suzuka Hanabi. She stared at her geta, red-faced. Imperial Summer had belatedly reached the Fuji Squad, and Hanabi was pacing nervously outside the manor, waiting for Kuon.

She hadn't been back here in ages. When her stepmother heard the news from Rin, she went wild and turned Hanabi into her own personal dress-up doll. Cloth was bound around and around Hanabi's chest and stomach, one yukata after another was put on and off, and her stepmother was never satisfied until Hanabi promised to wear it again next year. Ultimately, Hanabi managed to get her settled on a safe option. Even this one went for three times the average Jogen monthly income, so she wasn't really sure it qualified as "safe." Did it even count as a yukata anymore?

"Nnnnghh..."

But the thing she was least sure about was whether it looked good in the first place. Her stepmother and Rin approved of the outfit, and she was grateful, but since they both doted on her, she couldn't really trust their opinions. If she was wearing an expensive yukata that didn't even look good, Kuon-kun would think she was nuts.

That was all Hanabi could think about, so it never occurred to her to wonder what Kuon might be wearing.

"Senpai."

"Ku...Kuon-kun??"

When had he arrived? She'd been too busy staring at her feet and hadn't even noticed. She looked up when she heard his voice and was blown away.

"Sorry I'm late..." he said, embarrassed.

She'd just assumed he would be in normal clothes, maybe a yukata. He was not. He was in a hakama, with a haori over the top. Stunned, she managed to splutter, "D-don't worry about it..."

Why was he wearing that?

"Master put this on me. She said I should look the part if I was visiting the Motegi manor. And well...I'm the same height as her now, so..." He turned, showing her his back. The haori had a fan and seven stars on it—a family crest. "Apparently this is the Nanahoshi crest..."

Nanahoshi...the clan that had created the Shichisei Kenbu. "That's amazing!"

"It's a heavy burden on so many levels, and I feel like I'm cosplaying as a rakugo performer."

"Not at all! You look like a samurai! It's..." *Cool,* she started to say but was too embarrassed to get it out.

Kuon, however, had no such problems. He gave her a bashful smile and said, "Hanabi-senpai, that yukata looks amazing. You're beautiful."

She stared at her feet again.

_//////////

They were to meet up with the others at the Motegi's secondary building.

Next to the front entrance of the main building was a steep path. Hanabi and Kuon climbed that for a while and found themselves at the gate to the second building. There were several people up there, and one saw them coming.

"Oh! Kyuu-kun!"

Motegi Rin was the first to call out. She was the eldest

daughter of the manor's owners. She'd cut her hair a little bit shorter after they'd recovered the capital, and today it was in a braid hanging over her yukata's shoulder. When she saw Kuon's haori/hakama combo, she grinned.

"Kyuu-kun, what are you wearing?! It's so badass! You look like a knight or a shogi player!"

"Th-thanks, I guess..." Kuon said, sheepishly.

Rin turned to Hanabi, trying to make it look natural. "You agree, don't you, Hanabi?"

There was a long silence. Then Kuon thought he heard a click from inside Hanabi.

"Yes, it looks very good, Kuon-kun," she said firmly.

"Thank you, Hanabi-senpai!" He looked thrilled.

Rin shook her head. "She goes into Warrior Mode with everyone looking, and then she can totally say it just fine! Also, Kyuu-kun, you got the same compliment from both of us but sure took it differently."

"Er, I didn't mean to...owww!"

She gave him a noogie.

"Oh, where's Tooka-kun?" Hanabi said, as if just remembering. "I thought she was staying at the Nanahoshi home? Didn't the headmaster bring her?"

Rin had invited Tooka, too, naturally. But... "She's already asleep. She *is* only ten..."

Oh, Hanabi thought. "What about En-kun? Is she asleep, too?"

"She's with my Master. Something about swapping her body out for a new one."

"Swapping?" Hanabi looked confused. Then two people came up behind Rin.

"Looks like everyone's here," the man said.

"Squad Leader! And Nao-san!" Kuon exclaimed.

"Okegawa-kun. Nice hakama. Good look for you," Fuji said with a warm smile. One of the most handsome boys in the school, the breezy jinbei he wore looked all too good on him.

Next to him was a gentle, smiling girl, waving her hands. "Heyyyy! I saw Hanabi and Rin this morning, but Okegawa-kun, it's been ages!" She was Fuji's fiancée, Gotenba Nao. She was a third-year student and lived in the girls' dorm, next door to Hanabi and Rin. She didn't look the type but was excellent at mahjong...or, at least, cheating at mahjong.

They were all here. One high school boy, three high school girls, and one junior high school boy all began making small talk.

"Kyuu-kun, you've met Nao before?" Rin said, looking down at him.

"The squad leader introduced us once before," Kuon said, looking up at her.

"Rin! How long are you going to cling to Kuon-kun?!" Hanabi said, yanking him away.

"I think it's the first time we've all been together," Fuji nodded, only just realizing.

"Eh heh heh! You're all so close!" Nao said, enjoying herself.

Then came a rumble that echoed in the pits of their stomachs, and a beautiful flower exploded in the sky above.

Fwwwwwwwwwwwwww...boom!

There was a firework festival today. Rin's proposal had been that they skip practice and watch the fireworks. Not to slack off but to welcome their new teammate and strengthen the bonds between them with a little R&R. Sadly, the new teammate had fallen asleep.

"Ah! They're already starting!" Rin yelled. "Kyuu-kun and Hanabi were so late!"

"What? We weren't even supposed to meet for another twenty minutes."

"Oh, riiight... Which means..."

"Motegi-kun proposed the wrong meeting time. Honestly!"

"Jeez, Rin-san."

"J-just hurry! Before it's over! Come on!" Trying to cover up her mistake, Rin ran off, her geta clacking. The Fuji Squad, plus Nao, went out one of the back gates of the Motegi manor, through the gardens, and to the front of the second building. There, the servants had prepared seats for them to watch the fireworks. Hanabi had a firm grip on Kuon's hand, pulling him after her. Once they were all seated, another firework went off. Rin showed no signs of repentance.

This mid-September fireworks display was an annual Jogen event. The fireworks were launched from a park by the seaside and helped remind Jogen citizens that they were part of the Empire, even though they were a small island far from the mainland.

Since the Motegi estate was on a mountain with a fantastic view, there was nothing obstructing the colorful flowers blooming in the night sky.

"We've got lots to eat and drink! We'll keep it coming!" Rin said, playing the part of the hostess. Yakisoba and takoyaki were being carried to the tables nearby. This was Hanabi's home, too, so she pitched in, and when Kuon tried to join them they both snapped, "Children should sit down!" Finally, a giant tray of yakitori came out, and they were ready. Hanabi filled the disposable plastic cup in Kuon's hand with orange juice, so he filled hers with lemon-lime soda, and then he realized Rin, Fuji, and Nao were all drinking something brown and bubbly. Before he could ask if that was allowed, Rin proudly raised her cup.

"Cheeeeeeeeers!" she yelled, joyfully.

A firework exploded behind her.

Everyone tapped their cups together. Rin, Fuji, and Gotenba seemed to be competing to drain theirs fastest. Fuji had his hand on his hips, chugging like a post-bath milk, and Rin was standing on her chair letting it flow in, but Nao beat them both, sitting properly on her chair and holding her cup with both hands. They all flaunted their empty cups proudly. "Another!" At least wipe those moustaches off.

Kuon gaped at them, then his eyes met Hanabi's, and they giggled. Is it always like this? Pretty much. These words went unsaid.

"Cheers, Kuon-kun."

"Cheers, Hanabi-senpai."

The two members with non-alcoholic drinks clicked their cups together.

The rest of the gathering was wild.

The first five minutes brought a lot of memories back for Kuon. Possibly not even from his last life but ones before that.

Rin was as an awful drunk and was quickly berating Kuon, demanding to know why he'd taken Hanabi from her and what he was going to do about it. "Sorry, Kuon-kun," Hanabi told him. "She doesn't mean anything by it."

Fuji appeared to be in an excellent mood and then fell asleep after his third cup. Nao had drunk more than anyone else but wasn't even flushed. She pried the cup from Fuji's hand and softly kissed him on the cheek.

Ba-ba-ba-boom! The final fireworks went off.

The noise startled Rin, and she turned, falling out of her chair. This appeared to be all she had in her, and she just laid there, snoring. A butler appeared out of nowhere and carried her into the house. Fuji, too, was picked up by two burly bodyguards, and Nao followed them inside.

Which left Kuon and Hanabi all alone.

Kuon was unclear if this was Rin's plan all along, but now that they were free of the drunks, Kuon glanced next to him and saw his girlfriend's face lit by the fireworks she was named after. Like a waterfall, one flash after another, as dazzling as they were fleeting. Watching her watching them, Kuon forgot to breathe.

It was extraordinarily beautiful.

For some reason, he found himself thinking that at the moment of his death, he would remember how she looked tonight. "Hanabi-senpai," he found himself saying. He regretted breaking the silence. He'd wanted to stare at her forever.

The last few pops faded, the final lights dimmed, and a quiet darkness settled over them. Hanabi turned to Kuon and smiled. "What?"

This was a smile she reserved only for him. It hit him hard.

While the others were drinking and Rin was accosting him, their fingers had never untangled, like they were afraid to let each other go. Now he pulled her hand closer, making himself as tall as he could. He cupped her cheek with his free hand and tried to steal a kiss.

Clunk. He went in a little too fast and their teeth bumped.

"Oh!!" Both of them covered their mouths with their hands. It was definitely painful.

"Argh, Kuon-kun!"

"S-sorry..."

Hanabi snorted. Kuon hastily got on his knees on top of the chair, trying to make up for his failure. They had to do this properly. Hanabi's hands reached out, cupping his cheeks. Kuon didn't dare move.

She kissed him gently, their lips barely touching, and then she pulled away. He couldn't bear it. "I love you, Hanabi-senpai," he blurted.

She froze, startled. A moment later, her expression melted before his eyes. "Mmm," she said, a smile spreading across her face.

He just wanted to stay like this, and he believed in his heart that he was not the only one.

"I..." Hanabi said. "I want to stay like this forever, Kuon-kun."

There was love in her eyes. *Oh,* he thought. *That's how I feel.* He extended his knees, matching her eyeline. *I think this feeling is...adoration.*

Hanabi closed her eyes, and as his lips moved to hers, Kuon realized he'd found an emotion his previous life had never granted him.

_//////////¯

A few days later, the Lunatic Order were in a mock battle.

It was on their usual training ground, but there was one major difference. They'd merged training grounds one through three, creating a genuinely huge space. There was also one *other* difference.

"Suzuka-kun, the attacker at five o'clock is bait. So is the one next to it and the one in back. The real one is—"

"No, wait, Hanabi, don't move so fast, please, it's making me sick..."

"Senpai, I'll take the main attacker up above! Rin-san, take out the artillery for me!"

"Cut off the enemy retreat. Launch Servant Pods two seconds after Okegawa-kun's attack. Motegi-kun?"

"Wait, wait, I'll do it. Just wait... I had curry for lunch, and it's all coming up, so wait!"

A light shot across the blue sky. At the heart of this vast virtual battlefield, three figures clung to the back of a dragon. Shots flew towards them, but the dragon dodged as if predicting the future, dragging the attached three figures along with it.

Kuon, Fuji, and Rin were all attached to Hanabi's Kiryu.

Just as he did in the last battle, Kuon rode on the back of the Kiryu, cutting enemies as they approached. Fuji was working Control on the left wing, and Rin was on the right, trying not to puke while maintaining a one hundred percent hit rate one-handed.

"High Nova Launcher firing!"

Hanabi fired the Kiryu's main weapon, taking down two enemy gunners as they evaded the Servant attacks. Less than half remained. It was seven against one.

Not personnel—squads. Seven Lunatic Order squads—a total of twenty-eight Cavalleria—were all gunning for the Fuji Squad.

This was the Jogen Maneuver Academy Fall Exhibition Match, a Lunatic Order battle royale where everyone ganged up on the Fuji Squad.

The match had been planned by Headmaster Nanahoshi Kaede with the stated goal of knocking the Fuji Squad down a peg. Since they weren't satisfied by being permanently top ranked within the school, they'd gone and gotten themselves medals to boot. It all seemed familiar somehow, but she was their headmaster, so they'd lose the fight the moment they let themselves get upset.

Besides that, their real goal was checking on the adjustments to Hanabi's Drag Ride. Their new chief mechanic, Tooka Nürburg, had made considerable improvements to it. Given the operations scheduled in their future, they needed to put it

through its paces. "They're dominating, huh? Boring," Kaede muttered to herself, watching the battle.

Kaede's number one student raised a Blade to the sky. "Nine-count Strike! Kishin Ryuenbu!" A guillotine tornado sprang up. Cylindrical Blades each as large as a Jave raged, storm-like, across the battlefield around Kuon.

Hanabi's Kiryu alone had half-demolished them, and now Kuon used a Shichisei Kenbu area-of-effect attack to polish them off. He'd used the same technique in the Capital Gate Recovery battle to finish off nearly all the enemy Jave and save the Bushi Hime at the last second, so this art was particularly famous within the Air Force. The opposing Lunatic Order forces were taken down so quickly, one could almost feel sorry for them.

Only seventy-seven seconds had passed since combat began. Funds for the newspaper club—who ran the betting pool—were in great shape.

The Imperial Army's final goal was to seal all the Gates on the mainland. They'd sealed the Capital Gate, so that left thirteen more: Sapporo, Sendai, Yamagata, Ashinoko, Owakudani, Mount Myoko, Matsumoto Castle, Nagoya, Kyoto, Osaka Castle, Seto, Hiroshima, and Fukuoka.

The Empire would crush those Gates one by one. To give themselves a foothold, they'd chosen the Fukuoka Gate in Kyushu to start with. At the center of the operation would be their two heroes.

Expectations were particularly high for Suzuka Hanabi and

her Drag Ride. They'd poured a fortune into manufacturing the new weapon, and nobody wanted it turning out useless. Hanabi needed results as explosive as her name.

But while the manufacturing costs might be immense, the research and development had not been. After all, Tooka designed the whole thing herself.

Wheeling through the air, Hanabi glanced to the corner of the training ground. A small girl was looking up at her, donut in one hand. *She must really like those,* Hanabi thought. The taciturn genius child had nearly always had a donut on her since the day they met. They were easier to get than chocolate, but did all Shichisei Kenbu students have a sweet tooth? She had plenty of order rewards left, so maybe she'd have to bring more donuts tomorrow. It sort of felt like taming her with treats, but she wanted to do something for her cute "little sister".

The Heavy Magic Engine her sister developed was the core of the Drag Ride. Inside was the one thing that could store high-purity magic, the Crystal II, which Tooka had also invented. The system vibrated this magic, compressing it at high purity, and let it explode to produce energy. This explosion made the magic vibrate, so once an explosion happened, the engine had an inexhaustible supply of energy. However, that initial vibration required a twelve-second kick from a Division 5, and Hanabi was the only person in the Empire capable of that.

Hanabi had a lot of magic to begin with, and this system effectively doubled that, enabling her to use powerful weapons like the Servant Pods and the High Nova Launcher. But the most insane

function was definitely the Heavy Magic Field. By compressing magic and increasing its mass, deploying Heavy Magic around her unit, she could cause Jave bullets to slide off her. High-purity magic would even bend space.

This was impossible, according to everyone else working in DM development. But after calculations several hundred pages long and simulations run over a thousand times, the allies had granted permission for development of a prototype, and then Hanabi had proven its effectiveness in the last battle.

As long as they had the Heavy Magic Engine and Heavy Magic Field, mankind could finally win decisively against the Jave.

Whether the Imperial Army HQ was unanimously that optimistic was another matter. Tooka coming here was related. She'd requested it, but the allied forces' reluctance was likely a factor.

As a side note, using this Heavy Magic under certain conditions allowed one to intentionally overdrive things, causing the phenomenon known as Magic Dispersal. That phenomenon was at the heart of the Soryu Ranbu art Suzuka Hachishiki had used to blow himself up, as well as Kuon's ultimate move, the Mumyo Tosen.

Moves it had taken Shichisei Kenbu hundreds of years to develop had been achieved by Tooka in a mere ten. When Tooka first explained the principles of Heavy Magic, Nanahoshi Kaede's face had been a sight to behold, and it was a real shame no one but Tooka had been there to witness it.

This genius opened a window comm to Hanabi. "Hanabi-onee-sama, how's the Kiryu performing?"

As always, she had no expression, no emotion in her voice. Hanabi was getting used to that, though. "No problems," Hanabi said. "Actually, it's a little *too* good? Like, astonishingly so. I've got three riders, but the maneuverability is still better than before."

"I've tuned it to you specifically, so it should be responding like that. The more we link and synchronize, the more your magic and the Kiryu's Heavy Magic resonate."

"It's the strangest sensation... To me, it feels like the Kiryu itself is alive."

"That's an extremely healthy response. There's autonomously intelligent growth-type—NSR-type—AI Device functionality incorporated into portions of it, so it is absolutely 'thinking.' Even if it weren't, I personally believe all machines have a form of consciousness. Spiritual, electrical, or magical."

"Huh... Mechanics sure think differently."

"I think your perceptions are quite good, onee-sama. The test riders were not able to control Kiryu anything like you do."

"I'm glad I can help."

"You're being very helpful. The data you're providing is assisting with development of projects beyond the Kiryu."

"There're more?! This isn't the only project you're working on?"

"Right. I have three other projects supported by the Kiryu development. I suspect the international forces will brief you on them in the near future all because of the data you've provided. I'm grateful."

"Th-that's really... You're amazing."

"Thank you," she said, sounding both super earnest and entirely emotionless. Then the comm cut out.

Hanabi shook her head. But Rin, recovering somewhat from the motion sickness, said, "She's a lot like you, Hanabi."

"She is?!"

"You were just like that when you were her age! Super flat. Almost frozen."

"I was?"

"You don't remember?"

"I wish I knew more about Hanabi-senpai's childhood," Kuon said.

"Ah ha ha, I'll fill you in sometime. I got loads of juicy stories."

"Please don't, Rin. Kuon-kun, don't you dare ask."

Fuji jumped in. "I really didn't expect Motegi-kun to get motion sickness. Your extra weapon, Falcon, is also a high-spec mobility unit. Same as the Kiryu."

"Controlling it myself is totally different! Seems like I can't handle someone else at the wheel."

"Hmph... Interesting."

"But Rin," Hanabi said, "You've got to get over it. I can't exactly drive safe in combat."

"I know! I'm working on it..." Rin fluttered a hand.

"How long are you gonna jabber?" the headmaster cut in. "Wrap it up."

"Roger that!" The entire Fuji squad responded reflexively.

Then Kaede addressed all Lunatic Order members who had

participated in the mock battle. "Well done, soldiers. I've pre-pared a modest reward. Details in email."

Everyone thought the same thing: *This will definitely be hazing disguised as a reward.*

_/////////⌐

They weren't entirely wrong. The headmaster's "reward" was a barbecue on the Nanahoshi training ground/private beach. If it had *just* been a barbecue, it totally would have been a reward, but this was Nanahoshi Kaede, their headmaster, master of the Shichisei Kenbu. It wouldn't be that simple.

This beach was smaller than that of the Motegis—of course, the Motegi family's was an entire island, so they weren't even worth comparing—but the Nanahoshi beach was plenty big.

Big enough that thirty-two honed young Lunatic Order Cavalleria, the best the Empire had, were thoroughly worn out by twenty laps with the sand pulling their feet out from under them.

After a five-minute break, it also proved big enough for a beach volleyball tournament with four matches running at once, with a special prize from the headmaster to the winners, and the Shichisei Kenbu legendary punishment to whoever came in dead last. At the memory of the latter, Kuon and Rin started shaking so much they dropped their water.

The first match was Hanabi and Rin versus Fuji and Kuon. The final score was 21-2 in the girls' favor.

"Ah..." Holding a tissue to his nose, Kuon mulled over the

reason for their loss, not that there was any doubt as to that reason. Hanabi and Rin went off to their next match, their fit bodies squeezed into tube-top bikinis, doing fit jumps and fit attacks, and wow there was a lot of swaying up top. Fit swaying.

Their swimsuits were definitely very different from the last ones they'd worn—the one made of strings and the bubble nude-looking one. These were standard athletic tube-top bikinis. As such, they were highly functional, which itself really gave off the "fighter girl" vibe.

Kuon stared at Hanabi's taut thighs, the faint lines of her abs, boobs so big you could clearly see a deep valley which tube tops would normally not display, and the large behind that the bikini could barely contain, forcing her to constantly adjust the cloth. Everything had ridiculous amounts of jiggle, like something out of a retro fighting game. Even that was but a distraction compared to the depths of that valley, the sort of abyss that appeared to be looking back at you the more you stared at it, and thinking about that during the match as Hanabi spiked the volleyball and it turned sharply, the letters MIKE on the side coming—

"Ah, my nose is bleeding!"

His thoughts were dragged back to reality. He honked into a tissue, and the contents soon turned from red back to clear.

"I suppose you are a growing boy, Okegawa-kun." Fuji grimaced, also dabbing his nose with a tissue. He hadn't been distracted by the girls' bodies; he'd simply proved hopelessly terrible around balls. That must have been awful. Although he'd looked pretty happy when his fiancée Nao was tending to his injuries.

Speaking of tending to injuries...

"Onii-chan, are you okay?"

Tooka was right next to him, basically on his arm, serving as the Fuji Squad's manager/assistant. Her face was very close. She might be ten, but she was definitely very beautiful. Kuon's classmates might all be thinking, "Hot older girlfriend-having straight shota light novel MC, please explode!" but it still got his heart racing. He'd actually blown himself up in his previous life, so having people wish that fate on him behind his back was doubly cruel. *What was a "straight shota light novel MC,"* *anyway?*

"Uh, yeah, thanks," he said, realizing he had to answer his sister student.

"No need to thank me. I am your little sister. I'd do anything for you."

That phrasing really bugged him, though, and he wasn't her brother. "Sorry, Tooka-chan..."

"Call me Tooka."

Tug tug.

"Tooka, um...maybe not so close? This might be a bit of an emergency."

"Huh? Why?"

"Hanabi-senpai saw us and froze on the spot."

They heard Rin yelling, "Hey! Move, Hanabiiiiii!" as she did a flying save only to have her opponents mercilessly spike it back five millimeters from her fist.

"Ku...on...kun?"

He was, of course, seated right in front of her.

Last place went to Kuon and Fuji's team.

This was Kuon's fifth time, so he made sure to warn Fuji.

"Um, Squad Leader...do your best to keep your mind on something fun. Otherwise you will die."

"Die?!"

"Yes, but comms are active, so have Nao-san talk to you the whole time so you don't die."

"W-wait, what kind of punishment is this?"

"As long as you don't move too much, you'll be fine. Keep your breathing even so you don't die."

"You sound like a doctor releasing a terminal patient to enjoy his last days at home!"

"The water is our ally. The water is not our enemy. Keep your emotions level, so you don't die."

"Why is Motegi-kun shaking like a leaf?! Where does the water come in at all?!"

It would be a full day before Fuji was able to face a glass of water again.

When Kaede's hazing was done, the sun was setting. Having spent the entire day forcing the young to work out in the name of fun, the headmaster nodded her approval. "Glad to see everyone enjoyed their R&R. Well done. Time to roast some meat!"

Cries went up all around. Not cheers like "Yeehaw!" or "Yes!" but cries of relief like "We survived!" Like the walking dead,

they shuffled to the showers, changed into normal clothes, and their young bodies soon forgot how tired they were and got hungry instead. All their bellies rumbled. Their bodies craved meat. More meat!

At last, the barbecue was ready. There were ten tables set up, grills on each, to accommodate eight full squads—a little over thirty people. Fuji would normally take charge at a time like this, but he was down for the count thanks to the punishment. At the moment, he was in bed in the lodge with Nao at his side, so Hanabi took his place. Kuon became her hands and legs, making sure meat was delivered everywhere and there were enough plates and napkins. Rin watched, yawning, showing no signs of pitching in. The Cavalleria who had lovers with them turned some of the tables into couples' islands, and their blissful auras repelled the baleful stares from the boys and girls who were excluded. Kuon joined up with the Fuji Squad members, but Hanabi and Tooka each took a seat on either side of him and refused to budge, so Rin wound up sitting opposite him, her glare making him squirm.

Meat of all kinds was frying all around them. The party soon began and almost immediately hit a level of uproar that no one would mistake for sobriety. The Mitsuhashi squad leader was the first brave hero to slip some booze into the soda without the headmaster or teachers noticing. He was a foolish hero who pulled this trick every time, despite knowing full well the truth would come out eventually.

Those who started raising hell the moment their bellies were full were also fools. That group of fools—all men— tried to show

up the couple islands by standing on their chairs and playing rock-paper-scissors at the top of their lungs, the losers forced to strip.

Kuon looked askance at this terrifying male-only strip RPS game, with its cries of "Please, Mitsuhashiiiii, let me keep my underweaaaaar!" and such. He chose to stay focused on his tongs and the meat. That did not look like a fever to get caught up in.

Jogen beef was highly rated even outside their territory. *These islands were developed for grazing,* Kuon remembered. There were cows just wandering everywhere. The kalbi was particularly good. He flipped a steak on the grill, and noticed Tooka sitting with her plate empty.

"Meat..." she whispered, staring blankly at the browning fillet.

"Oh, sorry, Tooka, aren't you eating?"

"No."

"Really? Sorry! You can have this steak."

She shook her head. It didn't seem like she was being polite.

"Um... Did you get much steak in Germany?"

"Other people ate it a lot. I just...wasn't a fan."

To Kuon's right, Hanabi was eating scallops. She learned forward. "Not a red meat girl? We've got fish and shrimp, too."

Tooka shook her head again. "Just veggies."

Kuon and Hanabi, both interested only in beef, pork, chicken, fish, shellfish or any other meat, looked at each other. "Healthy!" they exclaimed.

"You two..." Rin said, shaking her head. She took a bite of marinated pork, chewed it well, and swallowed. "You're totally in sync over stuff like this! Like you're twins or something. Scarily close."

"Uh..."

"And now you're bashfully fidgeting in the exact same way, you happy bastards! Argh, I can't take any more of it! I'm going back to my room!"

"Wow, that's definitely a line that the first victim in a murder mystery would use," Kuon said, assuming that it was only polite for him to make a joke like that.

"Actually, I just forgot I had some wine back at the lodge, so I'm just going to get that."

"You're gonna drink again?"

Rin just fluttered her hands dismissively at the clueless children and left.

With a beautiful girl on his right and a beautiful child on his left, Kuon went ahead and put some onions, peppers, and pumpkin on the grill. Tooka's eyes locked on to them as if trying to fry them with her gaze alone. A shout went up from the next table. Hanabi was facing him and couldn't see, but her face was bright red, so she must have guessed what had happened. The Mitsuhashi and Sagara Squad men had forgotten the RPS game entirely and just all gotten naked. "Booooys, put those things awaaaay! We're trying to fry sausage over heeeere!" someone yelled. Hanabi buried her face in her hands. "K-Kuon-kun..."

"Yes, Hanabi-senpai?"

"Th-the first one I ever saw was yours so...that night was my first time..." *What the hell is burbling out of meeee?!* she thought in despair.

"Hmm?" Tooka stole Hanabi's cup and licked the brim. "Alcohol detected."

Seriously? Kuon thought.

Hanabi rambled on. "Kuon-kun, yours was...very...um... impress—"

"Aughhhhhh, Hanabi-senpai?! Are you drunk?!"

"Um, um, Kuon-kun, listen? Listen? I think Tooka-chan is..."

"Just Tooka, Hanabi-onee-sama."

"Since Tooka-chan got here I've been a little, just a little, a veeeeeery little bit ankshus but shtill, shtill..." Her speech was slurring more and more. Suddenly she grabbed him by his shoulders and gave him a huge smile. "But I love you more than anything in the world!"

So cute.

"Kuon-kun, I looooooveeeee yoouuuuu..." Her arms went all the way around his neck and held tight. She started kissing his cheek and neck. Kuon thought it was like Heaven but with an additional boozy scent. He settled for rubbing her head with one hand and wielding the tongs with the other. The veggies were about to burn.

Even in this situation Tooka was calmly saying, "Onii-chan, they're burning."

A breeze brushed by, feeling brisk on their cheeks. Kuon glanced up to find night banishing the last traces of orange from the sky. Too impatient to wait for the sun to set, stars began to twinkle. Nude boys were starting the world's most dangerous game of beach flags and fire limbo dancing, while he had

the most beautiful girl in school drunk and trying to make out with him.

This was Jogen Island, the last hope of mankind, and they were military trainees facing a seemingly endless war against the monsters. Yet in this moment...

It's peaceful.

He knew better. They all did.

This evening of fun would not last. It might never come again. Fear of the battlefield was always at the corner of their minds, a black pit of despair that made them want to scream. The Mitsuhashi Squad partied like they wanted to forget because just yesterday they'd finally found pieces of the female Attacker who'd died in the Imperial Recovery battle. The headmaster and teachers knew this, which is why they weren't stopping them. The other students knew it, too. Every one of them knew they could be the next to die.

But maybe they didn't really get it.

No one there thought that a month from now, two-thirds of them would be gone. That they'd have lost their chance to speak to two-thirds of their number.

No one knew.

One month from that peaceful night on the beach, the Student Echelon—commonly known as the Lunatic Order—would fall.

"Motegi."

A voice called Rin's name as she left the lodge, wine in hand. "Oh, Okayama?" she asked. "What's up?"

Okayama was an Attacker from the Sagara Squad. She'd gone up against him in several mock battles, and they'd been in the same class for three years running, so she knew him pretty well. He'd been learning Machine Fencing from Okegawa Kuon alongside the Air Force Cavalleria, too.

He was of average height and build. Neither tall nor short, neither handsome nor ugly. There was nothing particularly memorable about his appearance, but he smiled when other people didn't and picked up on the strangest things. When they were both second-year students, the Fuji Squad and Sagara Squad had stayed up all night watching horror movies in his room, and he would break out laughing when everyone else was scared, pick up on clues no one else did, and blurt out the identity of the killer, making everyone else punch him.

It had been kinda cool, so Rin had a comparatively positive impression of him. Like a tier below Hanabi, Fuji, Kuon, and En. Just then, though, he looked pretty serious. "Can we talk a bit? Alone?" he asked.

"Huh? Sure."

That was careless of her. Later, she felt like she should never have let him take her away.

He was a boy. She was a girl.

She didn't even think about that until they were around the back of the lodge, out of earshot of the barbecue revelry. There

was a look in Okayama's eyes that wasn't usually there. He looked super serious and really tense.

Stuff happened a lot in war. Especially in mixed-gender units; very especially ones filled with younger boys and girls. Girls could activate DMs too, but if their Device was stolen, what could they do? If she and Okayama started grappling, how could she fight back? She was a Sniper and he was an Attacker. She'd never stand a chance. She wasn't one for childish ideas like saving herself for the one she loved, but she hoped to at least have mutual consent.

She bluffed as best she could. "What are you bringing me over here for? Revenge for kicking your ass in that mock combat? Or are you gonna ask me out?"

She laughed out loud, trying to hide how scared she was.

That was a mistake.

Okayama silently took a step closer. Rin couldn't stop herself from taking a step back. *Uh-oh. Super uh-oh.* Alarms went off in her head, and she held her Device tight behind her.

"Yeah," Okayama said. "That's what this is."

"What?" she blurted out, having forgotten the thread of the conversation.

"Like you said... Don't make me say it. It's embarrassing."

"Huh?"

"I mean it, Motegi. I love you."

"What?" She couldn't understand him. *What is this? Is he really asking me out? Calm down. Wait. No, obviously. Of course.*

He was a boy, she was a girl.

And I'm a pretty hot one...so I guess asking me out was a possibility, too. Internally, she apologized profusely for doubting him.

"Motegi?"

"Um...right, okay. I get it. It's been a while, so you caught me off guard."

She'd actually been quite popular before high school. She was a Mote... No, never mind. But what now? She knew what he was thinking. "Um, Okayama...you...love me?"

"Yeah."

"Why?"

"Why...?"

"Not to say it myself, but I'm kind of a handful? Like, my personality?"

"I know. Three years in the same class and Lunatic Order stuff."

"Yeah, so why me? Not like you've been nursing a crush this whole time."

"Well..."

"You're a friend, so lemme be blunt. Just cause there are couples all around us doesn't mean you need to rush it. Half of them are just together to forget they're scared. You want someone for that, get some other girl. I'll hook you up."

"Like Suzuka and Okegawa?" he said, scoffing.

Annoyed, she snapped, "Not them. Don't be stupid."

"Ah ha ha ha ha ha ha!" Okayama burst out laughing.

What now? Rin thought. *What made this guy laugh?* "Is this a setup? Are there cameras rolling?"

"No, no. Ha ha ha, sorry. I take that back. Suzuka and Okegawa aren't like that. We all know that. Man, you really get worked up about Suzuka, huh? Normally you're the first to laugh."

"Of course I do! And I dunno about first..."

"I mean when you care about someone, you've got their back. You've been with Suzuka this whole time, helping her be a better fighter. It's because of you that she stopped being a headlong charge-in berserker and got as strong as she is, right?"

Yeah...

"You put your friends before yourself. You even warned me. So, like, I dunno... That kinda thing really caught my eye, you know? Once I picked up on it, I started seeing more, and before I knew it...I was in love."

She had no response to that.

"I thought you and Fuji were together for a while," Okayama continued. "Guess he's got no taste."

"I'd never go for someone so uptight, either. And I agree about his taste."

"I've got way better taste, right?"

"I dunno. But I'll think about it."

"Mm, sure. Oh, but...we don't have long till our next deployment. So...try not to take too much time, okay? If one of us died, that would really suck."

"I...I know that..."

"Then cool. Sorry I dragged you out here. Oh, and here."

Okayama pulled something out of his pocket and tossed it to her. She scrambled to catch it. It clanked against the DM Device

she was clutching in her hand. It was the key to a motorcycle. "This is the prize for..." she began, awed. The prize for the head-master's beach volleyball tournament were motorcycle keys. As one of the semi-finalists, Rin held the key in her palm, staring at it.

"Motegi, you like bikes, right?"

How did he know that?

"Your extra weapon, Falcon. Same thing, right? Long distance, high speed, mountable. And I ain't got a license so...that bike's yours. Gimme a ride sometime, okay?" With that, he turned and walked away.

Left standing behind the lodge, Rin, one of the semi-finalists, stared down at the key on her palm. "The guy's supposed to be the one giving the girl a ride..." she muttered. *Man...* she thought. *He really does love me.*

"Oh, I forgot..."

"Yikes! You scared the hell out of me!"

"This'll be hard to say if you gimme a no, so I figured I'd better say it now," Okayama said sheepishly. Just his head was poking over the wall. "You got a haircut after the Capital battle, right? I think it looks great."

"...Thanks."

She was not confident she managed to hide how red she'd turned.

_//////////

Later on that evening, the barbecue ended. The fools who drank so much they passed out were deposited in either the men's

or women's lodge, respectively. Cleanup had been taken care of, and everyone had gone to sleep.

One small boy staggered along on a dark path through the woods, away from the beach, away from the lodge, a wooden sword in his hand. Between the running and volleyball and water torture, he was thoroughly exhausted.

It was Okegawa Kuon. His master had summoned him for more training, despite how sleepy he was. As he reached the training ground, Kuon looked confused. "Huh?" he said.

There was a beautiful stranger standing next to his master.

She was wearing what looked like a silk kimono altered to be more cyber-chic, with long emerald green hair falling on either side of her. It was an eccentric look, to be sure, and she stared right at Kuon with a mischievous grin.

He looked at his master. "Um, who is this?"

"Check your Life Sight," she snapped.

"Can I?"

"Yes, go ahead." He'd been asking his master, but the new girl answered instead.

Huh, that voice sounds familiar, he thought, trying to remember where he'd heard it before. *Hmm...nope, too sleepy. Can't remember.* He just did what he was told and used his Life Sight.

Kuon raised both arms in front of him, laying the wooden sword along the horizon. He focused his mind, imagining himself wrapped in magic.

Machine Fencing referred to schools of sword techniques that were designed to make use of the magic channeled through

a Division Maneuver. Shichisei Kenbu was one such school. But what Kuon was currently learning were arts that used magic *without* a DM: Shichisei Kenbu's Eight Hidden Forms.

Those unnatural powers were as follows:

1st Form: Reject World.

2nd Form: Bubble Wall.

3rd Form: Crystal Cannon.

4th Form: Foresight.

5th Form: Void.

6th Form: Pleiades.

7th Form: Life Sight.

8th Form: Resonate.

These Forms weren't necessarily learned in order. As Kaede explained before, the qualities you were born with played a major role in how many you ever acquired. You needed talents unrelated to your Division.

Kaede had ordered Kuon to use one of these, the 7th Form—Life Sight. This ability allowed him to see the light of life, something the ultimate art, Mumyo Tosen, had allowed him to do. In other words, by acquiring the primary technique, he'd already learned one of the hidden arts.

The training Kuon had done so far enabled him to use Life Sight even without a DM, and he now used this sight to check out the mysterious cyber-chic beauty and see her light of life. Each person's magic was a different color. When Kaede first saw Kuon and said his magic was actually like her former student's, she'd been looking at the color of his magic. Kuon had only

recently worked that out. But when he looked at the cyber-chic beauty...

"Mm? Huh?"

"What?" Kaede asked.

"Maybe I'm still not good at this. But she looked exactly like someone I know only too well..."

"And who would that be?" the beauty smirked.

Kuon knew he was right. "So, uh...seriously? You're En?!"

"That's right, Kuon-sama!" she nodded, overjoyed. "You were being so dumb about it I was actually getting worried! But it's me, En!"

Yeah, she's definitely my master's former Device, all right. "What's with the new body?"

"It's amazing! Look at it, Kuon-sama! The Imperial Capital R&D team were developing this artificial flesh! Since we recovered the Capital, they resumed work on it!" En spun around, happily showing off her new form. He remembered hearing in his previous life that they were researching artificial flesh exactly like real bodies using a mix of cloning and magical technologies, but...

"The Imperial Research and Development Headquarters, was it?"

"Yes! The place I was born!"

"They've progressed this far? You're a full-on android now."

"If we put one on you, you would be a cyborg!"

"Thanks, I'm good," Kuon replied.

"If you lose an arm or a leg, just give them a call!"

"Perish the thought."

"Enough joking around," Kaede said with perfect comedic timing. "Kuon, continue from last time. Try Resonate."

In his master's opinion, the Hidden Form Kuon stood the best chance of mastering was Resonate. As the name implies, this literally resonated his magic with someone else's, allowing them to share it. As it was, it was possible to share a Witch Bubble with another person if they held hands, but he couldn't use it like his own magic. Resonate, however, would allow Kuon to use Shichisei Kenbu with someone else's magic.

"Once Nine-count Strike wears out, if you can use Resonate, your chance of survival increases a little. You'll still wind up getting saved by Hanabi, but..."

"I'll try to avoid that as much as I can."

"For today, En will be helping. Use her as you please."

"Kaede-sama, did you just turn me into a guinea pig?" En gave her master a shocked look.

Kaede just glared flatly back at her. It was strange hearing the two of them call each other by name. En hadn't even had a name before Kuon gave her one and had always called Kaede "Master" before.

"Never seen a light of life in an AI before. Seems like this one's genuinely weird."

"Is that a compliment? Should I take it as one, Kaede-sama?"

"Hmm, suit yourself."

"Yay! I love you, Kaede-sama!" En threw her arms around her former master, her new body far larger than Kaede's. Despite his master's stern expression, Kuon could tell she was secretly happy.

They were definitely close. Kuon grinned. "Here I go," he said. He turned the tip of his sword to the ground, holding it like he was standing upside down.

He took a breath and released it. *Focus. Focus.* Just as Life Sight allowed him to see people's magic, it also allowed him to see the magic flowing in the air. He imagined his own magic dispersing through that flow, as if disrupting it, and then he tapped the sword's tip on the ground.

Shichisei Kenbu Hidden 8th Form: Resonate.

A faint *tiiiiiiiii...nng* sound rang out. That was his own sound, like a submarine's sonar or a dolphin's echolocation. He strained his mind's ears so as not to miss the sound of En's magic that came bouncing back to him.

Tiii...nng...

There it was. This time he tapped twice.

Once again, he laid his own magic over the wave coming from En, keeping it even. Same speed, same angle, same depth. It was like if a ball were coming his way, and he threw a ball back with exactly the same force, aiming to make both balls fall at that exact spot. If he hit it head-on it would get knocked away. If he didn't use enough force his ball would get knocked back, but if he used too much the other ball would, but if he hit it just right...

...tiiiiiiiiiiiiiIIIIIIIIIIIIIIIIIIng!

This time he heard it clearly. En's and Kuon's magic were resonating. The light of life shone before each of their chests. This was visible even without Life Sight, a fact he gleaned from the surprise on En's face.

"Wh-wh-wha... Kuon-sama, this is amazing!"

"En...you're...Division 4? Wait, this isn't—"

"Well, yeah, I'm running on Kaede-sama's magic, so...."

"No, I-I-I-I-I know that, but..."

"Huh? What's wrong, Kuon-samamaamamama..."

"Uh-oh...ohohohoho!"

"Whaaaaaaat?"

Both stared shaking like they were being electrocuted. Grinning, Kaede said, "This is what happens when Resonance fails. You started off well but couldn't keep it in check."

"Heeelllllllllpppppppp!" they cried.

Kaede shook her head and then stomped her foot. Instantly, both Kuon and En gasped. Kaede's magic wave had intervened, and the resonance broke apart. *Such skill!* Kuon thought. "Ugh... I'm all numb..."

"Sorry...sorry..." En said.

"You've been using Hanabi and Tooka to practice with, but they're both Division 5, so they'd make Resonance even tougher to control." Kaede told them. "But I ain't subjecting myself to this! So En, this is your job now."

So heartless, Kuon thought.

En merely bowed her head. "Understood! I'll do whatever I can to make Kuon-sama into a great Cavalleria!"

"Cool."

"It's an honor to have my body be useful! Kuon-sama, use my body however you like!"

"Seriously, watch the phrasing," he complained.

"I won't let you sleep tonight!"

"Stop!" he howled. But a moment later...

"Unh..."

Both Kuon and En collapsed, completely out of energy. "Only stabilizes one out of every ten attempts...hmph..." Even with her Guide and student flat on the ground, Kaede was business as usual. She stared at them, evaluating. "Keep working on it."

A cool breeze brushed across the grass. Wrapped by nature's bedding, his limit long since passed, Kuon was sound asleep. En twitched a few times, showing no signs of getting to her feet. *See it through,* Kaede thought. Then she turned to someone else— the girl who'd arrived as the training was in progress. "I'll take the big one, you handle Kuon."

The little shadow bobbed her head. "Yes, Mother."

"Mm?"

A pain in his jaw woke Kuon. He felt a strange sensation, like he was dangling. Like a cat being carried by the scruff of its neck.

"Oh, onii-chan, you're awake?"

He turned towards the voice, and found Tooka on his right. She was wearing a DM for some reason. "What's going on?" he asked.

"I'm carrying you. Mother asked me to."

"Oh, okay."

The DM Tooka had activated had two massive exo-arms sticking out of the back, each absolutely large enough to carry a human. With these, Tooka effectively had four hands.

She herself was wearing a dress. The DM activation was localized to her back, and the giant arm carried Kuon like a cat, hooking the neck of his T-shirt and leaving him dangling in the air. His jaw hurt because the collar of the T-shirt was digging into it. He was lucky he hadn't suffocated. "Master didn't specify *how* to carry me?" he asked.

"Huh? No."

"Of course not." Kuon would much rather have been laid out on the palm of one of these giant hands but didn't argue the point. Instead... "Thanks. You can put me down now."

"Can you walk?"

"I'll be fine."

She put him down. He rubbed his aching jaw nonchalantly, trying to keep her from noticing. She was staring intently at him. "Wh-what?"

"Onii-chan, do you believe in past lives?"

This was sudden. But he had an answer ready. "...Master told me about you. I suppose we should talk a bit."

"Mm. Let's. I have so much I want to talk to you about."

She had no expression and didn't seem eager to talk at all, but he took her at her word. He glanced around. They were pretty close to the lodges.

The Nanahoshi private beach had three lodges, a main one and two smaller ones. The smaller ones were divided between the students by gender. Kuon and Tooka were near the women's lodge. He could hear whispers from the dark forest around them—couples, most likely. He decided it was best to move

farther away. There was a rocky area on the way to the main lodge. Hoping there was no one already there, he suggested the location to Tooka, who nodded.

"Onii-chan...hold my hand?"

"Sure, okay." Given what Kaede had told him of Tooka's past, he couldn't exactly brush her off. Besides, it was dark, so they started walking hand in hand. Her tiny hand was soft and warm.

They walked in silence for a time, away from the buildings, past the path leading down to the beach. They reached their destination. No one could see them from above. The night sea lay before them.

Tooka sat down on a large rock. Kuon sat next to her. "I guess we should pick up where we left off. You're..." He glanced sideways. Tooka was staring up at him, no emotion visible in her eyes. His heart shrank, but he forced the words out. "You were Suzuka Hachishiki's little sister?"

Tooka Nürburg nodded.

_/////////⌐

A few decades back, in Tooka Nürburg's previous life, she had been Suzuka Hachishiki's little sister. Her name was Akigase Tooka.

Hachishiki himself hadn't know this, but his mother got divorced shortly after he was born. She married another man and had Tooka with him. Tooka's mother and father were only a year apart in age, but Tooka's father got sick and died when she was two.

When Tooka was five, her mother was struggling financially. She asked if she could return to the Suzuka home with Tooka in tow. Hachishiki's father had agreed to this. But...

On the way home from the meeting where they'd arranged this, they were attacked by Jave. Both Tooka and their mother went missing. Hachishiki's father had been driving them home and was believed to have died along with them.

Akigase Tooka had only lived five years.

Before her death, Tooka and Hachishiki had played together, but only once, on the day she and their mother came to ask for help. But Hachishiki had forgotten it and had never been told she was his sister. Hachishiki had no memories of his parents at all. His memories began after his arrival at the orphanage.

Meanwhile, Tooka was reborn.

At first, she didn't know that.

Five years ago, a girl had been found lying at the gates of Nürburg Castle. She had almost no memories—all she knew was that her name was Tooka and that she was the heir to the Shichisei Kenbu.

On this last point, Kaede had but one word: "inexplicable." The day Tooka died, Kaede hadn't even met Hachishiki yet. Tooka and Kaede had no point of contact in this life or her last. It was possible she learned of the Shichisei Kenbu in the five years of this life that she'd lost, and these memories had been mixed with those of her previous life.

Still, Kaede was unable to ignore Tooka and had taken her in, splitting her time between the Empire and Germany. Tooka's

talents had soon become clear, and the Germans were not about to let her go. Kuon had long wondered why his master was so busy despite having no students in her private school, so this certainly cleared that up. She'd been looking after Tooka.

Then a month ago, things had changed.

Right after the Imperial Capital Recovery, the battle that had earned Kuon and Hanabi the Twin Star Heroes name, Tooka saw Kuon's face on news coverage of the disappearance of the eastern capital Gate. "My brother!" she cried. Her memories returned.

Not memories of this life but of her past life. Memories of somewhere clearly not here, of a time clearly not now, and...of her mother and her own death.

However, Tooka was too intelligent to just accept these memories as fact. They were impossible. They didn't make sense. But they were too vivid to dismiss as a dream. Plus, if she was from the eastern Empire, that would explain the color of her skin and hair. Using her memories, she investigated what records she could find. The more she investigated, the more real it seemed, and it frightened her.

At last she made up her mind and told Kaede everything, including her memories of being Suzuka Hachishiki's sister. Kaede looked unusually surprised...and then confirmed those memories were real.

The truth was clear. Tooka had been reincarnated twenty years after she'd died in her previous life.

Tooka was forced to accept this as fact. She resolved to visit the Empire, using the in-progress development of the Kiryu as an

excuse. She felt that the Kiryu's rider being a Suzuka, as well as her brother's girlfriend, showed the hand of destiny at work.

Tooka Nürburg was finally here.

"I was Suzuka Hachishiki's sister in my previous life. And you were..."

Kuon nodded back. "I'm Suzuka Hachishiki's reincarnation. And I guess that does make you my sister."

Tooka's eyes seemed to glisten. "Before my memories returned, I always felt like I was looking for someone. A boy about my own age. One who'd been nice to me. But I couldn't remember who," Tooka whispered. "I was so lonely. I had no memories, so I felt like I couldn't even prove that I was myself. I always felt like I was watching someone else's life go by." She paused. "Then I remembered you, onii-chan, and I knew that wasn't true. I finally understood. I was the sister of the Hero, Suzuka Hachishiki. That must be why I was a Division 5, why I knew so much about Division Maneuvers. That gave me the confidence. Put my feet on the ground. I was really me." Tooka looked at Kuon. "I was so happy," she said. He caught the faintest glimpse of a smile. "For you, I'll do anything. That's the reason I was reborn."

"For me?"

"If you fight for the people of the Empire, then I'm here to help with that. If you want to make Hanabi-onee-sama happy,

then I'll help with that. I won't get in the way. But...but if you want a child with me, just say the word."

"I'm gonna pretend I didn't hear that last bit. Uh...thanks."

Expressionless, she leaned in close. "That last one was the most important."

"Please don't."

"That was a joke. Was it funny?"

"It was hard to tell you were joking!"

"When you were reborn, did you have your memories?"

"Um...yeah, I did. I died inside the Gate and immediately after that I was a baby. My memories transferred to Okegawa Kuon's body. Although I lost my magic..."

"That's strange. I have the same body and magic, but you have a different body and different magic."

"I thought I was reborn because I was inside the Gate...but you never were?"

"I really don't remember. We were in the car, then everything went black...and that's where my memories end," she told him.

"Maybe you were Division 5 then, so they took you into the Gate..."

"I read that report. That's why they took Hanabi-onee-sama through, and then you risked your life to save her. That was wonderful, onii-chan."

"Th-thank you."

"Hanabi-onee-sama's wonderful, too. She's beautiful, and strong, and really understands the Kiryu, and gives me lots of donuts."

Like a pet, Kuon thought wryly.

"I'll work hard. I'll make the Kiryu stronger, make lots of other frames, and the Jave—" Tooka suddenly froze mid-sentence, as if her batteries had just run out. Her mouth and eyes were both wide open.

"Tooka...?" Kuon said cautiously.

She blinked and began to move once more. It were as if she'd just rebooted. "...Sorry, I fell asleep. I'm usually in bed by now. What was I saying?"

"Um, you'll work hard..."

"Right. Let's work hard together, onii-chan."

Kuon nodded "S-sure..." What on earth was that freeze about? Something was definitely off. Their conversation ended there. They went back to the lodge and went to sleep.

Despite that bit of weirdness, Kuon's world was still at peace.

_//////////⌐

That same night, Hanabi woke up with a hard pillow under her left cheek. She was lying on some mildewy sheets. There was no sign of any covers.

She realized she was in the women's lodge. The beds were all in rows like in a field hospital. She was at one edge of the room, and everyone else was asleep. Cramming a bunch of sixteen to eighteen-year-old JK—delicate, fragile creatures—into a single big room was *so* Nanahoshi Kaede. Of course, these girls were neither delicate nor fragile, so it was totally not an issue. As proof, they were all sound asleep.

But Hanabi was freaking out a bit.

She didn't remember anything.

She remembered Rin going to get some wine. Then she wanted a drink herself, and she knew Rin would get mad at her for it, but Kuon was with her, so she figured it would be fine. She slipped a little castle town Napoleon into her soda and drank that, then talked to Kuon...and then she couldn't remember anything else. She really wanted to believe that the part where she poured out her heart to Kuon and then kissed him a lot was a dream.

There was a video message on her Device. She was almost afraid to open it. When she did, she found Kuon looking apologetic. Like a prisoner waiting for a death sentence, Hanabi set it so only she could hear. But it was just a simple "You fell asleep so I carried you here." She looked around. Several beds were empty. Probably off flirting, the hussies. She had a boy of her own; why was she wasting time sleeping? Hanabi felt really sad.

"...I'm thirsty," she whispered.

"Oh, Hanabi!"

As she chugged a sports drink from the vending machine by the main lodge, a friendly voice called out. "Nao!" Hanabi said. "What's up?"

Nao came over, smiling and waving. She had a couple of boxed drinks in her hands, so she was probably here for the same reason. Nao glanced towards the dark forest, from which they could occasionally hear whispered conversations or...other sounds...and put her hands to her lips, giggling. "Everyone's getting carried away, huh?"

"We all went to war and looked death in the face. Can you blame them?"

"You feeling lusty yourself, Hanabi?"

"Er...well...yeah."

"Ah ha ha! I was kidding! Sorry, sorry. So you going to find Kuon-kun?"

"Nooo...probably not."

"Really?"

Hanabi quickly deflected. "What about you?"

"I'm with Jin-kun, of course! We haven't had any trysts or anything yet. He wants to wait till we're married. Jeez... He's got a girl like me and won't do anything? Pfft."

"Ha ha, that sounds like him."

Nao stared at Hanabi's face for a moment. "...You seem softer these days, Hanabi."

"Huh? I'm still working out!"

"I mean personality-wise. You're more...relaxed? Compared to last year you aren't talking like a bushi nearly as much."

"You think it's...?"

"Kuon-kun's influence? Or is that pushing it?"

"I-I dunno. I'm not really conscious of it, myself."

"But you're blushing!" Nao reached out and rubbed her head. "Oh, I saw Kuon-kun headed that way earlier."

"Wh-which way?"

"There," Nao pointed behind the main lodge. Hanabi thanked her and started walking. "Oh, but...he might not be alone... Too late, huh?"

Hanabi was already out of earshot.

It was the worst possible timing.

Hanabi found Kuon by the rocks. She was about to excitedly call out to him when she saw Tooka with him and realized they were holding hands. She was instantly crestfallen.

"Oh..."

She wanted to call out, but this didn't seem like something she could interrupt. She also lacked the courage to do so. She crouched down on the rocks above them instead, hiding where they wouldn't see her. *What now?* She fidgeted, listening to them talk.

"You were Suzuka Hachishiki's little sister?" Kuon said.

Hanabi nearly froze. *Tooka-chan is the Hero's sister?!* That didn't make sense. He died thirteen years ago, and his parents long before that, and Tooka was only ten and...

Below her, Tooka nodded. "I was Suzuka Hachishiki's sister in my previous life. And you were..."

He was...what? What was Kuon, then? Thirteen years old, Lunatic Order, Twin Star Heroes, best Fencer in the Air Force, successor to the Shichisei Kenbu...

...Wait.

Thirteen?!

Shichisei Kenbu?!

She never noticed before how strange a coincidence that was, but now it was spinning through her mind. Before she could even sort it out, Kuon spoke.

"I'm Suzuka Hachishiki's reincarnation," she heard him say. "And I guess that does make you my sister."

This time Hanabi really did freeze.

What did he just say?

She was pretty sure even the blood in her veins had stopped flowing. *He has to be joking,* Hanabi thought. *Kuon is just playing along with Tooka, who is clearly into spiritual mumbo jumbo like past lives and destiny or whatever. I mean, there's no way...*

Kuon was talking again. "Um...yeah, I did. I died inside the Gate, and immediately after that I was a baby. My memories transferred to Okegawa Kuon's body. Although I lost my magic..."

That can't be true...

Hanabi tried to laugh it off, but her own memories were revolting. During the Capital Recovery, after the two of them went in the Gate, what had En said?

"Your memories will be transplanted into a baby somewhere. Essentially, you'll be reincarnated."

That meant reincarnation was an actual possibility. Not fiction but something that really happened. People were actually reborn.

She shook her head. No. Even if that was a remote possibility, and that did happen to Tooka, that didn't prove the same thing had happened to Kuon. He must be making this up based on what En had said, piecing it together from one fact or another. She was sure that was the case.

Hanabi staggered to her feet. She couldn't call out to him now. It never even occurred to her to check with him what the

truth was. She just wanted to get away. The longer she stayed listening to them, the more real it would seem. All her doubts would fall away, one after another. The more she thought about it, the more certain she'd become.

So she had to move. She couldn't think about it.

She knew that instinctively. This was not something she could let herself know. Kuon's mysteries, strange behavior, odd maturity, frightening skills, all of that...all of it pointed to *him*. It wasn't true. It couldn't be true. She couldn't let it be true, because if...

If he really is the Hero, I'll never forgive him.

If Kuon had been lying to her this whole time, knowing how much she looked up to the Hero...what greater betrayal could there be? So it couldn't be true. He was just making it up.

She told herself that over and over, all the way back to her bed in the lodge, where she didn't sleep a wink.

The next day, back in her dorm, she told Rin about it, like it was a big joke. Rin looked serious for a second and then broke out laughing. She laughed so hard she was crying. "Still," Rin said, "That's waaaay too dumb. Better not tell anyone else."

Her eyes weren't smiling.

Hanabi felt like that was a warning. *Oh,* she thought. *Even Rin thinks so.*

Okegawa Kuon might really be Suzuka Hachishiki's reincarnation.

ONE WEEK LATER, three weeks before *the day*...

Hospital wards always had a distinctive scent. Not as pungent as the men's dorm but sweeter than a person's natural body odor—the kind of smell that makes you sleepy. It felt like burrowing into a futon someone else had just vacated.

It was three o'clock in the afternoon, the middle of visiting hours. Kuon walked alone down a corridor on the sixth floor of the Jogen 3rd Municipal Hospital past patients and nurses alike. There were large rooms on either side with the occasional door standing open. He glanced in one, and his eyes met those of a random old lady. He quickly averted his eyes and moved on. This was where these patients lived. He shouldn't stare.

He arrived at the room he'd been directed to and found the door closed. There were six name tags on the door. Her name was on the top right, indicating the bed in the back on that side.

His master had given him a fruit basket that screamed "hospital visit." Holding the basket awkwardly, he slid the door open. The beds at the front on either side had curtains drawn,

the middle beds were vacant, and the bed in the back on the left had an old lady chatting with a woman who looked to be her daughter, facing a TV window together. In the bed to the right was Hanabi, engrossed in a book. Kuon immediately knew which book it was. "Um..."

"Yes?" She looked up and saw him. She blinked a few times and then stammered, "K-K-K-K-K-K...!" She pointed at him. It almost sounded like she was laughing, but she was just super surprised. "Kuon-kun!"

The "Kuo" part was particularly loud and the rest almost a whisper. Kuon thought it was adorable.

She hid the book behind her and then frowned, "Wh-why are you here? I said not to come..."

His master had specifically warned him not to say that she'd sent him. He showed her the fruit basket, feeling a little awkward. "Um...well...just thought you could use some company."

"Thanks. So the headmaster told you to come, then?"

"Yeah... Oh..."

"You're too honest for your own good, Kuon-kun," she said reproachfully, but then she giggled. She was in her pajamas and her usual ponytail was down, so she looked like she'd just woken up. She was in the hospital, so of course she looked like that, but given how she usually maintained that gallant older girl vibe, seeing her hanging out in pajamas was a real turn-on for Kuon. He wanted to hop into bed with her.

"What are you looking at?"

"I want to curl up alongside your pajamas, Senpai. Oh..."

"See? Eyes up here. And you oughta call ahead before you come see a girl in a hospital."

"Sorry." He bobbed his head. Every time he apologized, he got scolded for not meaning it, but he'd learned that if he bowed his head, he was less likely to cause misunderstandings.

"Fine." Hanabi nodded, satisfied. Case in point.

Then she glanced behind him and bowed her head. He turned to look, and the elderly patient and her daughter were both looking their way, whispering to each other. "I knew it was her! Who is she?" "The one from the TV."

Kuon managed a strained smile and said, "Hey," as he closed the curtains.

Hanabi made a sulky face while clearly not being the least bit upset. "Aw, it's your fault they figured it out."

"Sorry."

"No use."

"How can I get you to forgive me?" he asked.

"Well... Oh, bring the fruit closer. Wow, she gave you a good one! That must weigh a ton. You can use this chair. Rin broke that one the other day..."

Hanabi laughed at the thought. She seemed in good spirits and pleased to see him. He hoped his coming here had brightened her day. Hanabi rummaged through the basket. "I love melon," she said. Or maybe it was the melon, then. "You can't just show up all sudden, Kuon-kun! My hair's a fright! I'm so ashamed."

"Sorry."

"But I'm glad you came."

She grinned at him. *This isn't fair*, Kuon thought. *How many times was she going to make me fall in love with her?*

"Wanna get in bed with me?"

"Yes—er, no! I'm really sorry!" She giggled at his fluster. He was glad to see her well. But after a brief silence, he asked, "Are you feeling all right?"

"I'm fine now. Sorry I worried you." She grimaced. Kuon tried not to look at the bandages on her left arm. "You had to save me again."

"No, I..."

Five days earlier, Hanabi had been injured in the battle for the Fukuoka Gate. She was sent to an Imperial military hospital and then transferred here. Military hospitals were always full, so patients in good condition were soon sent to civilian facilities. The fact that Hanabi was here after less than a week proved it wasn't a serious injury.

Kuon thought back to what had happened...

Five days earlier, during the Fukuoka Gate Battle...

The single Lunatic Order squad participating was the Fuji Squad. Hanabi wore her Division 5-only new weapon, the Drag Ride, and was once again dropped from the sky directly towards the Gate.

"Heavy Magic maximum output, all weaponry engaged. Nova Gravity Bomb deployed."

A microsun dropped from the heavens towards the Jave mantas swarming protectively over the Gate. Before the Jave even saw the Kiryu, the Ultra-Hot Bullet burst right above the surface, a blinding light evaporating everything around it. It melted them, turning them to ash and blowing them away. In one instant, the Jave on the surface, the eggs laid in the town, and the four Meat Pillars were all gone.

The Kiryu was still wheeling through the sky above, observing the world below. The Jave outside the blast radius came swarming in, but there was no sign of the Queen emerging from the Gate. That was a first.

Thirty seconds after receiving this news, command ordered the Kiryu into the Gate. While dodging manta attacks 20,000 meters above the ground, the Kiryu and Air Force Cavalleria raised objections and arguments against sending a Student Echelon squad into an unknown dimensional portal solo. However, command ignored them, repeating the orders.

In her usual tone of voice, not sounding put out, Hanabi asked, "Squad Leader, what now? Going into the Gate is one thing, but there's no telling what'll happen inside. We go too deep, we might not make it back."

"We've got our orders," Fuji said grimly. "If we sense danger, we'll just have to turn back then."

"Okay, okaaay," Rin said. "Roger that. Kyuu-kun, you cool? You gonna look after Hanabi and us?"

"I got you, Rin-san. You handle the ranged foes."

Fuji nodded. "Everyone ready? Suzuka-kun, take us in."

"Copy that. Drag Ride and the Fuji Squad entering the Gate!"

The Kiryu dropped down. Kuon was strapped onto its back with a cable arm. He knelt, drawing his Blade.

Inside the Gate was a place like outer space, and there was a welcome party waiting for them. Hundreds of tentacles emerged from the void, stretching towards the Kiryu. Kuon breathed out.

Shichisei Kenbu: Mod. Tensetsu Shigure.

Time seemed to stop. Enemy attack routes and evasion routes were shared with the Kiryu, along with everyone strapped to it. What the Kiryu's large frame couldn't dodge, Kuon cut down. Rin shot the tentacles just outside that range. Fuji located the Queen, and Hanabi shot a single extra-wide bullet ahead of them which burned everything in its path. They'd done exercises like this in training and mock battles any number of times.

Time moved again, and everything played out as planned.

"Queen located! Two o'clock above us!" Fuji shouted.

Kuon sliced and Rin shot and Hanabi launched her bullet, turning the Kiryu's head towards their target. The blast lit up the starless space and struck the massive conical lump of flesh. The Queen screamed as her skin, muscle, and bone burned and melted, finally evaporating away.

Screeeeeeeeeeeeeeeeeeeeeeeeeeescreeeeeeeeeeeeeeeeeeeeeeeeeeeeeeeeeeee!

The Queen let out a roar that hit the pits of their stomachs and made them want to clap their hands to their ears. It was an inhuman, ugly, revolting noise that pulled up Hanabi's memories

of the Capital battle and her childhood trauma, and made her thoughts and body freeze.

But the magical lines connecting her to her squad reminded her that she wasn't alone here. Her courage bolstered, she let out a roar that shoved aside everything worming its way under her skin. Kuon and Fuji and Rin all screamed with her, their spirits and vigor rising. The voices of her friends on her DM's back gave Hanabi's quivering fortitude the push it needed. The whole team's hearts were one, and the bullet she fired ripped into the Queen's massive bulk, about to eliminate it entirely.

Nothing happened.

The bullet ripping straight through the enemies inside the Gate suddenly vanished.

On her monitor, Fuji yelled, "Heavy Magic Engine offline! Shit, the field'll—"

A moment later, the Heavy Magic Field surrounding the Kiryu vanished. The tentacles fired a shower of light bullets at the defenseless Fuji Squad. Kuon stopped time, but not only were there no evasion routes, the magic link was cut and he couldn't share anything with his squad. Time flowed again, and he blocked three bullets with his Blade before it shattered. He'd managed to save his three companions, but...

"Retreat! Run for it, now!" Fuji ordered.

Hanabi was struggling to do something about the Kiryu's stalled engine. At Fuji's shout, Rin broke off firing at the encroaching tentacles to yell, "Hanabi!"

A number of light bullets struck the Kiryu's bulk, exploding.

Hanabi ejected a moment too late. Her Witch Bubble protected her, but the blast sent her flying. Rin instantly deployed her extra weapon, Falcon. She shifted it to Riding Mode, hopping on and chasing after Hanabi into the void.

"Senpai! Rin-san!" Kuon shouted.

"Change of orders!" Fuji said over the comm. "Okegawa-kun, kill the Queen! Leave Hanabi-san to Motegi-kun!"

"But..."

"Just kill the damn thing!"

"Ah...!" Before another thought struck him, he activated Tensetsu, found attack routes, evasion routes, and approach routes, and as Tensetsu ended...

Shichisei Kenbu: Chijin.

Three quick shukuchi and he was at the Queen's side. Using up so much magic that fast left him feeling like all of his blood was rushing the wrong way, and he almost threw up. His heart was beating unnaturally and his vision tunneled, but he pulled his other Blade and prepared to thrust.

Shi...chisei Kenbu: Mumyo Tosen...

Direct hit.

Magic Dispersal activated, and the Queen's body began to crumble. Hearing her scream, Kuon used the last of his power to push away towards his friends.

Huh?

He couldn't feel his body. His vision went black. He felt himself floating, stretching, falling, on and on and on and on and on and on and on and on and on and on and on and on and on and

on and on and on and on and on and on and on and on and on and on and on and on, and then it was gone.

Suddenly he felt pressure all over his body. It took a moment to realize it was the familiar sensation of Earth's gravity.

He opened his eyes. His gaze flickered over white curtains, a white ceiling, bed rails, and tubes from an IV. His master was holding the hand with the IV in it, her eyes swollen and staring at him.

"...Uh?" Why was she here? Where was he?

His voice wouldn't obey him. No sounds came out. *It must be really worn out,* he thought. All he could get his voice to do was make little "ah" and "uh" noises. As he wondered why, Nanahoshi Kaede spoke up.

"You're a fool."

His master was stricter than any demon, yet here she was starting to cry again, having clearly cried far too much already. That bad? So bad even she cried? What had happened? What was going on?

What happened to me? The Squad? Hanabi?

A wave of panic ran across him. Hanabi had been blown away. What happened to her? He couldn't just lie here. He tried to sit up.

"Calm down, Kuon," Kaede said, pushing him back down. She wasn't letting him fight her, yet her touch was still gentle. "They're all safe. Hanabi, too. Don't worry."

What happened? Kuon thought again.

Kaede began to explain. Right after the Kiryu went into the Gate, the veteran attacker squads who'd been learning Fencing from Kuon managed to finagle orders to investigate, entering the Gate.

(How? Through sheer annoyance. "Sorry to bring this up on open comms, Colonel, but didn't I see you at a singles café in town the other day? Sorry I didn't say hi, but don't worry, I won't tell your wife. Oops, I failed to make it clear which colonel I'm talking to! There're so many people at command with that rank... huh? We should go into the Gate and investigate, you say?")

Inside, they found no sign of the Queen, but apparently they did come across an injured Bushi Hime with no Kiryu; the sniper who'd saved her; their Fencing instructor, who was uninjured but unconscious with a pulse so low he was on the brink of death; and a squad leader looking ready to die himself, dragging their instructor towards the Gate.

Kuon had been unconscious for a full day. Hanabi was transferred to a civilian hospital right away. Tooka was investigating the cause of the Heavy Magic Engine stall. It was important to know why, since it had nearly wiped them out.

"Now, Kuon..." his master said, having explained everything. Her glare had a powerful rage behind it. It felt like the temperature in the room had dropped by ten degrees Celsius.

In short, Kuon was pretty sure he was about to die.

"Soryu Ranbu," she said. "That's a forbidden art, and I'll regret telling Suzuka Hachishiki about it into my next life...but you do understand why Mumyo Tosen is the ultimate art, right?"

"Because it's so powerful?" he rasped.

"If you evade another question, I will kick you out."

You know the real answer, he admonished himself. "Because using it too often will kill me."

Right. Shichisei Kenbu's ultimate art, Mumyo Tosen, was an art that caused Magic Dispersal inside a target, but it also took a considerable toll on him. During the battle, waves of that Dispersal came back up the Blade to him—faint waves but unavoidable. The wind of death both blew away his target and damaged his own light of life. That was why he'd been knocked unconscious. The Magic Dispersal had struck him right as he was nearly drained from using Chijin three times in rapid succession.

Mumyo Tosen guaranteed its target's death, but the price for that was a portion of the wielder's life.

His master had made sure Kuon knew that. After the Capital battle, he'd been reminded of it again while swinging a wooden sword as punishment for ignoring her orders not to use it. There was no excuse this time.

Kaede sighed, half angry, half resigned. "You really do love sacrificing yourself. You haven't learned a thing since your last life."

"You always say death can't fix stupidity. But..." He didn't tell her that he didn't want to die. She knew that without him saying so.

"Listen, Kuon. Don't try to do it all yourself."

"If I stop trying, then Hanabi-senpai will be the one doing that."

"Is that why you didn't tell Fuji or the army about the price of the ultimate art?"

"That and it just seemed like a pain in the ass."

"You're talking like En now. Where do you two get that from?" Kaede muttered. Probably from her, when she thought about it. "Anyway, you are not to use Mumyo Tosen again without my permission."

"If I do, will you kick me out again?"

"No," she said, averting her eyes. "I won't. But I won't forgive you, either."

That sounds worse, Kuon thought. But the next thing she said was even harsher.

"If the Shichisei Kenbu I taught you kills you a second time I'll never forgive myself."

Kuon had nothing to say to that. He didn't dare even look up, not allowing himself to see her face. He just stared at her hands.

They were unmistakably the hands of a sword master. But today, they looked so much smaller.

They sat for a long time in silence.

_//////////

After he was released from the hospital, Kuon got a message from Hanabi telling him not to bother visiting her. He was worried and wanted to see her and thought about it a long time, but then decided to respect her wishes and went to practice. His master looked at him like he was an idiot and immediately said as much. "You're an idiot," she said a second time. "Just go!"

After that it was all a blur. It took him an entire day to figure out which hospital she was even in. As the Empire's sole Division 5, the school's strongest Cavalleria, and the adopted daughter of the Motegi clan, her personal info was appropriately secure, but really Rin-san could have made this really easy if she'd have just told him.

Meanwhile, his parents started asking if he would think about quitting this whole Cavalleria thing, and he had to insist he'd rather die than do that. Tooka took a break from investigating to come and apologize, and she started crying so hard that he had to comfort her.

After all that had settled down, Kuon started thinking way too hard about what to bring with him to see Hanabi. He tried to choose some flowers or sweets or a book she'd like and wasted way too much time on that. Before he knew it, he was standing outside the hospital, holding the fruit basket his master had given him. It wasn't until he actually opened her door that he realized he should have called ahead and told her he was coming.

Now he was in front of her, staring at her bandaged arm.

"You were in bad shape, too," she said. He'd been released two days before. "But thanks for coming."

"No, I was just...asleep. And I managed to kill the Queen, so... it's all good."

Hanabi looked dejected. "I had no idea Mumyo Tosen was that bad for you. You should have said something."

"Sorry..." He hadn't wanted to worry her, but that wasn't his place to say.

"Um, Kuon-kun," she said hesitantly. "Is there anything else you're hiding from me?" There was an anxious look in her eyes.

I was Suzuka Hachishiki in a past life. He nearly blurted it out. "Er, um...no...?" His tendency to just confess to anything really made this tough, and he was definitely acting really suspicious.

Hanabi gave him a long, serious stare. "...Really?"

"R-really," he stuttered.

"Okay, then. Sorry."

"S-sure."

"But, yeah… Mumyo Tosen is really strong but comes with a price. That means we can't just make you bail us out every time. I've got to be better."

"No, I'm fine, honestly."

"And we definitely need the Kiryu. I'm worried about the engine, but…"

"We still don't know why the Heavy Magic Engine stalled."

"Yeah, unfortunately."

"Tooka came to see me yesterday. She's really sorry this happened."

"Yeah. She came here, too. Things just go wrong sometimes. We made it back alive, and the operation succeeded, so I told her all's well that ends well, but…" Hanabi glanced at Kuon. "I dunno, it's hard to believe she's really a kid sometimes. Same as you."

"Ah ha ha…" He figured this was because they both had been reincarnated, but he couldn't say that. Although in Tooka's case, her mental age really was about ten.

He felt like he was hiding more and more things from Hanabi, and this was really driving him into a corner. The ground was crumbling beneath his feet.

At any second he might fall.

That evening...

Hanabi lay in bed, stroking the cover of the book in her hands—a biography of Suzuka Hachishiki called *Portrait of the Hero*.

Hanabi was well aware that Kuon was hiding things from her.

She was glad he'd come to see her. She'd asked Rin not to tell him what hospital she was at, but he figured it out anyway. She felt bad for making him jump through hoops. She just...hadn't wanted to see him and have it be awkward.

Hanabi knew why the Heavy Magic Engine stalled during the Fukuoka Gate Battle a week earlier. She'd told Tooka as much the day before.

As the bullet was about to swallow up the Queen Jave, she was certain she heard a voice...

"Queen located! Two o'clock above us!" Fuji shouted.

As soon as the Kiryu fired, Hanabi turned its head in the direction he indicated. After vaporizing the Queen's tentacles, her next shot struck the wall of flesh. The Queen screamed as skin and muscle and bone burned, melted, and evaporated.

Screeeeeeeeeeeeeeeeeeeeeeeescreeeeeeeeeeeeeeeeeeeeeeeeeeeeeeeee!

The Queen let out a roar that hit the pits of their stomachs and made them want to clap their hands to their ears. It was an inhuman, ugly, revolting noise that pulled up Hanabi's memories of the Capital battle and her childhood trauma, and made her thoughts and body freeze—but the magical lines connecting her to her squad reminded her that she wasn't alone here, giving

her courage, and she let out a roar that shoved aside everything worming its way under her skin. Infected by it, Kuon and Fuji and Rin all screamed with her, their spirits and vigor rising. The voices of the friends riding behind her gave Hanabi's quivering back the push it needed. The whole team's hearts were one, and the bullet she fired ripped into the Queen's massive bulk, about to eliminate her entirely...and then Hanabi heard a single word echoing in her mind.

Wrong.

A moment later, the engine stalled. It was over in a moment. She couldn't do anything.

Hanabi realized what she'd heard now. That was the Kiryu's voice. The will of the Kiryu, born within the Heavy Magic Engine. She did not meet its approval and knew exactly why.

The one thing connecting both the Capital Battle and her childhood memories—the Hero—gave her pause. Could she really put her faith in the Hero? Could she really trust him, even as she merged her strength with his? Deep in her heart, a tiny, tiny part of herself was whispering, planting the seeds of doubt. Her link with the Kiryu transferred that, and it did not approve. The Kiryu's goal, its reason for existing, was to kill as many Jave as possible.

Tooka had seen a strange waver in the Kiryu's data and agreed with her hypothesis. The control systems had an AI Device of the same type as En, and if they added speech functions, it might start talking.

It'd probably give her a piece of its mind. It was mad at Hanabi. Really mad. It thought she was an idiot.

"In the middle of a battle, I lost faith in my companions, lost focus, and nearly killed us all." She said it out loud to drive it home.

How horrible.

Tooka had said, "I'll discipline it for not obeying its rider's instructions," and she certainly would. Even if the problem with the weapon was fixed, Hanabi's problem remained. If she couldn't eliminate her doubt, she'd make another blunder someday.

She should have just asked. Just put it out there. *Are you the Hero?* Plain and simple.

"Kuon-kun..."

She buried her face in her knees. Hanabi simply couldn't find the courage to ask that question.

_/////////

One week later, two weeks before *the day*...

"So quiet," Rin said sleepily. She was on the couch in the Fuji Squad meeting room. As she'd said, the entire Cavalleria building was silent. Everyone was out on a mission, so it was almost unoccupied. Only the Fuji Squad members in the meeting room remained: Fuji, Hanabi, Rin, and Kuon. They all wore their Maneuver plugsuits with the school-recommended windbreakers over them. They looked like members of a track team.

Hanabi was sitting at the monitor desk in the center of the room. She turned back to Rin and said, "Hey, we're on standby for this mission! No loafing around!"

"Yeah, I know..." Rin said, waving her hand. She appeared to be melting into the couch. Next to Hanabi, Kuon grinned at this familiar riff, and Fuji considered scolding Rin himself but abandoned the idea.

Hanabi's injury was mostly healed, and the bandages were only still on her arm as a precautionary measure. The broken bone and burns were fully healed within a week—the Witch Bubble and modern medicine were really impressive that way.

The Fuji Squad's two main attackers might have both been injured, but looking at the big picture, the last operation had been a huge success. After all, they'd eliminated a Jave Queen and a Gate without any fatalities. There were only two injured, a prototype frame badly damaged, and minor damage to the Reimei frame. They were the most miraculous results since the war with the Jave began. Despite the ambush, this was a far better result than the four-figure death toll the Capital battle had incurred.

Rumor had it that as a result, the Fuji Squad would be showered in medals and guaranteed significant ranks once they officially joined the Air Force next year... That is, if they survived that long.

With this success behind them, the Fuji Squad were left out of the current operation so the Twin Star Heroes could rest and recuperate. They were ordered to be on standby, but that was mostly a formality. No one was checking in on them, so they could hardly blame Rin for not taking it seriously.

The monitor desk showed the view from the mobile mothership's cameras in real time. It displayed blue sea and sky, with the occasional white cloud—Aohime Island. Specifically, the

Mid-Blue space, where the Imperial Air Force had closed a gate and the Kiryu had first seen action.

The Air Force and the Lunatic Order were deployed there en masse, but not because new Jave had appeared. This operation was entirely an experiment. They were testing a new Device developed by the genius researcher, Tooka Nürburg.

"Is this even possible?" Kuon said, voicing everyone's thoughts. "Can we...make our own Gate...?"

There was a long silence. The very idea seemed stupid, but it was theoretically possible. The method was, naturally, an application of Heavy Magic, but Kuon had stopped comprehending the explanation less than ten seconds in. As far as he was concerned, it was like a spell. Like, abracadabra extra veggies garlic with that?

But Kuon thought it sounded worth a shot. The space inside the Gates was merely a passage; they could get in but not go through. Many people had gone into the Gates, but nobody had gone out the other side and returned to tell the tale. To open the door on the other side required a different key.

And Tooka was trying to make one.

Ideally, this would take place somewhere a Gate had already been. That meant the Capital, Fukuoka, or Aohime Island. Of course, there was no need for this to take place in the Empire. There was no telling what would happen in the event of a failure, and they were opening a door to the world of their mortal enemies, so it could likely lead to combat. However, the military and imperial top brass had settled on Aohime Island.

This was because, unbeknownst to the Cavalleria, this

operation was being run by the international alliance, and the Empire currently owed them one. They couldn't argue with them about it because military command had ordered the Kiryu, *on loan* from the alliance, into a Gate...and lost it. To make up for that failure, they were forced to agree to an obviously risky plan like manifesting a Gate over their own territory.

Technically, the entire Kiryu hadn't been lost. The most important part of the frame, the Core, was recovered safely by Hanabi before it exploded. As long as they had that, it could easily be repaired and reconstructed. Such was the magic of Division Maneuvers. Naturally, the alliance hadn't told the Imperial military this. Hanabi had reported it, but somewhere along the line the information had been deliberately suppressed, and it hadn't reached the right people.

So now, the students sent to help with the experiment were gathered in the sky over Aohime Island. They were holding specialized equipment similar to curved metal poles. Linking these together made a massive ring, like the frame of a mirror or window.

Fuji pointed at the screen, explaining, "Supposedly the Gate will appear inside that ring, but that's just a support material. The DM with the capacity to make the Gate is—see, here it comes."

It looked like a pitch-black egg.

On the screen, next to the flying mobile mothership, they saw an even bigger elliptical object. This DM was like an egg painted black on its side, but it wasn't paint. This was a Heavy Magic Field, bending the light so it appeared black. The Servants flying

around it were cameras, the eyes of the user inside. Since light couldn't get in, they couldn't see out, either.

"This is the Anti-Jave Combat Final Mobile Maneuver, the Nürburg. Naturally, it's Division 5 only, and the rider is Tooka Nürburg-kun. The frame itself was developed as a final weapon, but in this instance, they're using it to open a Gate."

The sheer scale of it got Rin off the couch. "That's huge! Ridiculously huge! Bigger than the mothership! That's, like, the size of our school!"

Hanabi and Kuon were equally stunned.

"Wow...it makes the Kiryu look tiny..."

"And Tooka's inside that thing?"

The DM that was big enough to rival a Queen Jave slowly descended into the ring. The ring itself seemed to have thrusters on it and was hovering unsupported as the students backed away.

The countdown to start the operation hit zero, and the Nürburg began to move. The field around it began rotating irregularly. The pitch-black surface changed, alternating bands of white and black like a zebra, and then the white began to dominate. A black dot appeared at the center, surrounded by white. It looked like a single black point at the center of a white egg.

Then the black dot was gone completely, only to reappear at the center of the ring.

To Kuon's eyes, it looked like the dot had moved from the Nürburg to the center of the ring. The ring began emitting light, shifting dizzyingly from red to green, green to blue, blue to yellow—and then the black dot in the center *cracked*.

That's when it got really wild.

A black, sticky fluid-like *something* spilled out of the black dot. But rather than fall towards the ocean, or spill over the edge of the ring, it instead filled the ring itself like it was trapped inside transparent glass. Once full, it swallowed up the black dot as well. All that was left was a black mirror of darkness. Everyone watching recognized it, thinking the same thing: *It's just like a Gate.*

While everyone stared at the black mirror, wondering what would emerge, Tooka stood on top of the Nürburg, her DM deployed. It was the same exo-arm type of DM she'd used to carry Kuon.

"What is she—"

Tooka approached the mirror and reached out with one of her exo-arms, touching the surface.

Wump.

Ripples ran across the mirror's surface. A beat like a heart echoed, and the waves turned to a swirl. As the spinning grew faster, black sparks started flying around. As the sparks grew more dramatic, a black shock wave shot out of the mirror. The screen went completely blank, but soon restored itself. By then...

"She did it!" someone whispered.

At the end of Tooka's exo-arm was a 300-meter-wide, one-centimeter-deep black field, spinning like a black hole.

"A Gate...!"

The same black moon that had brought mankind to the brink of death had now been created by mankind's own hands.

What happened next was perhaps inevitable.

With the pseudo-Gate opened, Tooka turned her back on it, heading back to the Nürburg. Suddenly, a flood of Jave poured out from the other side. The manta swarm turned 180 degrees and wheeled around the pseudo-Gate, attacking Tooka, the Nürburg, the Student Echelon on standby behind that, the Air Force Cavalleria, and the mobile mothership.

The battle had begun.

The feed on their screen cut out. "Squad Leader!" Kuon yelled.

"Emergency deployment!" Fuji orders. "Everyone, activate your Maneuvers!"

Halfway out the window, Hanabi turned back. "We don't have orders yet, though?!"

"They'll come in on our way! Let's go!"

Hanabi kicked off the window sill, activating Reimei in mid-air. Kuon and Fuji were right behind her. "Rin!"

"S-sorry...!"

Rin was the last to leave, looking unusually rattled. Aside from the Fuji Squad, the entire Lunatic Order was in this operation. That included the Sagara Squad, and their attacker, Okayama. Hanabi had heard about Okayama and Rin's budding relationship, so she put a hand on Rin's shoulder and whispered, "He'll be okay."

"...Yeah. I know." Rin nodded and mounted the extra weapon on her back—the long-distance movement unit, Falcon—like a motorcycle. The other three grabbed onto the end of it, and all

thrusters fired, accelerating rapidly. In the blink of an eye, the school was out of sight.

Command ordered the Fuji Squad into action two minutes later.

_//////////

Tooka's consciousness faded to black.

The mantas that flew out of the Gate had her surrounded in no time. Like sharks circling their prey, they wheeled around, above, and below her. The sheer number of them blocked the sunlight, and everything within the sphere of mantas went black. Fear made every hair on her body stand on end, leaving her paralyzed with horror. One manta turned towards her, tentacles reaching out...dozens of them, hundreds of them.

She felt like this had happened to her before.

She couldn't remember when. The tentacles wrapped around her like a cocoon. Only when her vision was completely cut off did Tooka finally scream. Dark red Jave tentacles tightened around her arms and legs, binding them, and more tentacles with warts on them went in Tooka's mouth and ears and nose probing...

Stop   please

H...help

<Who?>

Everyone

_//////////⌐

She felt like someone...
Some*thing*...
Laughed.

_//////////⌐

In the end, everyone lived. Everyone who participated in the Aohime Island Pseudo-Gate Opening Operation survived intact.

The mantas that swarmed the squads never attacked the Cavalleria. They simply flew past and went back into the pseudo-Gate. Once they were all back inside, the Gate closed behind them.

By the time the Fuji Squad got there, everyone was preparing to leave. It was as if the Jave had never appeared at all. That was partly because experienced soldiers weren't rattled by a little trouble, but...naturally, it wasn't that simple.

Tooka Nürburg was taken to the medical ward, where she remained unconscious. She was uninjured and appeared to just

be sleeping. Had her experiment been successful? They had not managed to cross over to the other side, but the Jave's appearance proved that a path across had been made. That meant Tooka's research could progress to the next stage. Namely...

"We invade their world?"

In a briefing room on the mothership Tooka and the Sagara Squad had retreated to, Kuon was being brought up to speed.

"Yes. First step is armed reconnaissance," Fuji said after taking his drink's straw out of his mouth to answer. "We'll be using the pseudo-Gate created today, along with the final weapon, the Nürburg."

The large screen in the briefing room showed an aquarium filled with all sorts of digital fish. Naturally, there weren't any manta.

"And we'll be included in this mission?"

"Likely. Two weeks out, at the earliest. Oh, Sagara-kun, you okay?"

The Sagara Squad were filing in, and the squad leaders began talking. Kuon had been training one of the attackers on this team, Okayama-senpai. Just as Kuon remembered that, he saw Rin break off her conversation with Hanabi and head over to said attacker. She looked a little awkward. He'd heard they were class-mates, but this seemed different.

"Kuon-kun," Hanabi said, coming up to him. Even with that windbreaker on, she couldn't hide how large her breasts were. Her lower half was still in a skin-tight plugsuit, so half her butt was still visible, and her thighs—

Hanabi suddenly crouched a bit, placing herself at his eye level.

"Ah!" Kuon gasped. "Sorry, Senpai! What is it?"

"I guess boys don't *just* like boobs. You really like everything, huh?" She sighed, shaking her head. Yes, he definitely liked all parts of her body. "And here I was going to clue you in on Rin getting a little romance of her own."

"Rin-san is?"

"See her with Okayama-kun? He asked her out."

"Wow...he asked Rin-san? What, really?!"

"You seem a little too surprised. Everyone else already knows."

"Ugh, gossip never seems to reach me. This is when the gap between classes—or between high school and junior high school—really shows itself."

"You're his Fencing teacher, right? I guess students and teachers don't talk about that stuff."

"Did Rin-san agree?"

"She hasn't given him an answer yet. I'm glad he's safe."

"Yeah...really."

They nodded at each other. Both of them watched Rin and Okayama talking.

Rin handed Okayama a drink, being a little more curt than usual. "You hurt? Kyuu-kun's Fencing help out at all?"

"Not hurt. I think...it helped? Less wasted movement?"

"Yeah, I thought the same thing while I was watching. Uh, not just you! I was watching all the attackers."

"I know," he said with an awkward smile. Then it turned into a mischievous grin. "You actually saved me, you know."

"Huh? How so?"

"I mean, if you'd given me the okay, I'd have been all, 'If I make it back alive, let's get married!'"

"You idiot." This came out way nicer than she'd expected, and Rin panicked a little. Her worries had all melted away and now there were tears in her eyes, so she got even more flustered. She pretended to adjust her glasses to hide wiping her tears. "The Lunatic Order takes those death flags and cuts them down," she said.

"That only goes for the Fuji Squad."

They both laughed. *Oh, good,* Rin thought. *We can still laugh like this together. We're both still alive.*

In that moment, she'd already found her answer. Later, she'd be glad she didn't say so out loud, given what happened afterwards.

"Okayama, let's go," the Sagara squad leader said.

"Okay!" Okayama said. "Then I'll see you tomorrow at school," he told Rin and left the room.

Not a line you hear often in the belly of a mothership, Rin thought. But she waved after him.

Their lives were still normal.

A week later, a report came in that multiple Gates had appeared over Europe. Nearly all territories had fallen.

It was no longer possible to get chocolate.

That was because the fall of Europe had messed up the sea lanes, but most Jogen residents didn't know this. The news was only showing the exploits of the Twin Star Heroes and the success of the Pseudo-Gate Operation nonstop, and that information was being strictly regulated.

Kuon was kept very busy with scouting missions towards European lines that had dropped out of contact, Jogen ocean patrols, and Air Force Cavalleria Fencing lessons. When he arrived home for the first time in a week, he found his parents waiting for him on their knees.

"Sit down," they said with uncharacteristic solemnity. They had a form in front of them for withdrawal from his school. What followed was a complete breakdown of communication between parents who had only ever known peace, and a Hero who was on his second trip through hell.

"It doesn't make sense for a thirteen-year-old boy to be kept away from home for an entire week!" his mother said, worried. "And if your heart stops again like last time, I will absolutely die!"

"Let's move to the Capital," his father said gravely. "If not there, Kyushu. You've worked hard enough."

Kuon looked appalled. *The Capital?* he thought. *Fukuoka? Don't be ridiculous. They're still extremely dangerous!*

He'd been worked so hard this week his brain was barely functioning, and he struggled to find a way to convince them. *Mom, Dad, we can't; it's too dangerous. Not just the Empire, but the entire planet, our entire world...and I'm just too sleepy.*

Whatever, he thought. *I'll just show them the videos from Europe.* He'd recorded these himself, but Fuji, Hanabi, and Rin had all seen the same thing.

What they showed was hell on earth.

The video started with them crossing the Mediterranean near the base of Italy's boot. Even over the ocean, they could tell the land was on fire. The sky glowed red, covered by swarms of black mantas. One of those swarms saw them and attacked. You could hear Fuji reporting in to command. The screen was seventy percent enemies and thirty percent red.

His mother fainted during the mid-section. He kept it playing. It showed what happened after landfall in Sicily. It was awful. There were towers made of half-eaten humans. One of those "humans" was a land Jave in disguise, and one ally Cavalleria got too close and got the entire upper half of his body bitten off. When Kuon cut that Jave in half, a number of heads rolled out. That was when his father ran for the bathroom, his hand clapped over his mouth.

In the last and most extreme section, the Fuji Squad was forced to decide whether to abandon fifteen children standing right in front of them in order to rescue 3,000 refugees on an escape ship ten kilometers away. Hanabi, crying, was unable to make up her mind. Her DM dropped out, and she crouched down. Kuon, knowing full well this could get them all killed, proposed the stupid idea that they split the squad in two. Rin agreed with him, and Squad Leader Fuji accepted it. Since they couldn't save the 3,000 refugees without Hanabi's Servants, they

left Kuon alone with the children. They spent thirty hours hiding, trying to avoid being found by the enemy, but by the time the rest of the squad returned, there were only six of the fifteen children remaining. While Kuon was watching this, his father came back from the bathroom, found Kuon crying his eyes out, and gave him a firm hug.

This was a mistake, Kuon thought. *There was no need to show them this.*

He'd lost count of how many times Hanabi had cried this week. On away missions, she spent all night with her arms around him, and Kuon learned how to rub her head in his sleep. During downtime, he often found Rin with her arms around her knees, staring at nothing. Fuji would have a window open and appear to be diligently writing a report. When Kuon realized he'd actually been picking a wedding dress for Nao, it was genuinely unsettling. No bride wanted an Oiran-style dress!

They laid his mother down in bed, put a damp towel on her forehead, and then Kuon finally ran out of steam. He remembered his father carrying him to his room and putting him in bed. In his dreams, Hanabi was crying and hugging him, so he rubbed her head.

Ultimately, closing Gates one at a time was meaningless. The Twin Star Heroes were winning battles, but mankind had been given a harsh reminder that their enemies were infinite. They had to strike at the root of the problem: their hive.

Reeling from Europe's loss, the Alliance bet everything on a plan to send Tooka's final weapon through the pseudo-Gate and

destroy the Jave's world. This weapon was called a Magical Black Hole and was explained to Kuon—who gave up on understanding it after three seconds—thusly:

First, two Gates with a Heavy Magic radius would be overlaid, creating a space where they would endlessly bleed into each other. Once anyone went inside, there was no way out, only an endless Gate interior. After it was activated, it would grow into a powerful gravity pull that would swallow up everything around it, and one second after the sixty-minute mark it would expand faster than the speed of light. The expansion area was relative to the Heavy Magic radius and, depending on settings, could grow large enough to swallow a solar system. Once it passed the critical point, it would collapse at the same speed it expanded and vaporize, leaving nothing behind.

If that black egg which was the Nürburg self-destructed, it could create an artificial black hole. It sounded absurd, but apparently this was humanity's last hope.

Some members of the alliance and Imperial command were of the opinion that no matter how much was at stake, destroying an entire solar system was going too far. "Were" being the operative word. The fall of Europe silenced them. Ever since the war began, there had been a strong belief in certain portions of the population at the civilian level that the Jave were sent by God to punish mankind for destroying the environment, and they should accept these angels and allow themselves to be destroyed. Naturally, this viewpoint was ignored. The current belief the world over was "kill or be killed."

But their lives went on. They still had homes.

After twenty-four hours off, Kuon was back at school.

Europe had been horrific, but class was super peaceful. The spiky-haired kid he'd fought in the mock battle during the entrance ceremony brought over a motorbike magazine and was all, "Yo, yo, Okegawaaa, dude, this V-Twin is badass, right? Right? You know it is, that senpai of yours was all riding this crazy cool bike the other day. I bet that thing's a new model, lucky!" and showed him a bunch of pictures. Kuon didn't get much studying done, but he took a make-up test designed for Lunatic Order members.

The history lecture was on the Ancient Roman Empire, and this felt like such a sick joke that he started laughing, which was bad. He remembered what happened in Sicily again and locked himself in the bathroom, which was bad. He'd forced a whole meal into his stomach, but now his breakfast was all over the toilet and he felt like his heart was turning into Suzuka Hachishiki's again. He'd been through his share of hell in his previous life, and even *he* was this messed up by the aftermath of Europe's fall, so Hanabi and Rin and Fuji must be really bad. Was Hanabi okay? Was she crying again? He'd have to go check on her later.

Hanabi, like most of the soldiers who'd been on that scouting mission, was getting mental health care at the military hospital. She was told that it was far easier to develop PTSD far away from home—especially given her childhood experiences—

as opposed to in battles she knew would be protecting her home-land. Nevertheless, she went to school in the afternoon, sitting in class 3-A with Fuji and Rin and Nao and Okayama, earnestly listening. The concept of "college exams" literally didn't exist for her, but she felt she needed at least the minimum level of educa-tion expected of an Air Force officer. Then she realized she was five years older than Kuon and started wondering just how much she'd outrank him by the time he was allowed to formally enlist. Giving him orders not as a senpai but as a commanding officer sounded fun. She let her thoughts dwell on a future that might not ever come.

Their lives went on. They still had homes.
Until the time came.

At the time, Tooka Nürburg was sleeping in the alliance mobile mothership's medical ward, but she woke up screaming. She had all her memories back and knew exactly what was com-ing. *No time!* Her Device, Mother, onii-chan, she had to call now, now, now, where was her Device, out of bed, legs collapsed under her, cut her lip as she fell and her blood was red and that was a relief.

At the time, Nanahoshi Kaede was in a seat on an airplane on her way home from Europe, her first sleep in thirty hours. En was sitting on her shoulder, back in her original small body, organizing the intel gleaned over the last few days. A call came in

on Kaede's Device from Tooka, who'd been sleeping on the alliance mothership. It seemed urgent.

At the time, Rin was in class 3-A, half-listening, trying to decide how to answer Okayama. She'd thought about him a lot on their scouting mission. When Hanabi was curled up with Kuon instead of her, she'd felt so weak. Having someone to rely on might help. She'd have to talk to him after school. Where, though? Give him a ride on her bike to Mount Suribachi? You could see all of Jogen Island from up there, and only the Motegi family were allowed in, and you needed a bike or car to get there.

At the time, Okayama was staring at the back of Rin's head, a few rows ahead and to the right of his desk. When she asked what he liked about her, he hadn't known what to say. Really, he just liked that she was weird. And sometimes very fragile. Gunning for the eldest girl in the formidable Motegi clan was pretty scary, but the way she was lately, he couldn't just let her be. He wanted to protect her.

At the time, Fuji was looking over his left shoulder at Nao, desperate to see her in a wedding dress. He'd been on the fence for ages but decided he preferred Western style over Japanese traditional looks. Nao in a pure white bride's veil would be the most beautiful thing in all the world. They would talk about her in the world to come. He would have to find an artist to paint her portrait. Once they got married, they should have lots of children. Two boys and two girls. Never a quiet moment. Such fun.

At the time, Nao had narrowed it down to two venues and was trimming the fat from the budget. She knew Fuji would want to make a spectacle of it, the times be damned, and had been fussing over what dress she would wear for ages. She knew he'd want lots of children, and no matter how old he got, he'd never beat her at mahjong, and she was absolutely certain she loved him more than anyone else.

At the time, only Kuon noticed that their last three hours had begun.

_/////////⌐

Kuon was in class in room 1-A when he felt a chill run down his spine. He leapt to his feet, glaring at the ceiling. Everyone turned to look at him. Spiky-hair was all, "What's up, Okegawa? Siddown!" But Kuon wasn't listening. Something was coming. No...something was here. His instincts were screaming *pull back!*

Still unsure, he deployed his Maneuver against school rules, used Tensetsu, and saw all evasion routes pointing straight backwards. Looking around, he saw thick lines heading downwards from above, and then Tensetsu ran out. As time resumed, he screamed, "Everyone, activate DMs! *Now!*"

An instant later, there was an ear-splitting crash. The ceiling ripped open, desks exploded, the window glass shattered, and his classmates' heads turned to mist. This happened all around him, following the lines he'd seen with Tensetsu.

When Cavalleria were attacked, DMs automatically deployed, and the Witch Bubbles that deployed along with them tried to protect their Cavalleria, but there was a brief delay before it happened. In most cases, this was fatal. Only the spiky-haired kid and a few others reacted in time, but given what happened next, perhaps they'd have been better off dying right then.

Screams shot up everywhere.

It all happened so suddenly, nobody could grasp it. The classroom was demolished. *It hurts, help, they're all dead, call for help.* People were screaming the names of friends who'd lost half their bodies; people standing stock-still, unable to process things; people trying to pull the rubble away, everyone in a panic. Not one person was calm enough to assess the situation, including Kuon. But he'd sensed that these were Jave light bullets.

A rain of Jave fire had landed on their school. He didn't know why or what would happen next. When that thought hit him, he started shaking like a leaf. "Shit. Everyone, run! To the Cavalleria—no, to the maintenance bay! Take refuge there!"

It was too late.

First, a sound like an earthquake and a shock wave shook the school, the sound of multiple large things falling around them. Then a scream came from the floor above, DM Rifle bullets began firing outside, and black things swarmed out of the sky towards them. When they got close enough, tentacles reached into the hole in the ceiling and snatched up one of his classmates. She screamed, there was a horrible *splat*, and then the sounds of blood and flesh dripping.

"What...?"

"No...no..."

"This can't be happening...not here..."

The surviving classmates all stared up. As they did, a massive form fell into class 1-A, shaking everything. It was a blob of dark red conical flesh covered in eyes and mouths, with tentacles everywhere, like a hideous defective monster.

"Aieeeeeee!"

A land Jave had appeared right in front of them. These kids weren't Lunatic Order. They were just cadets, barely six months into their training, barely different from your average first-year junior high student. They'd never seen a Jave in the flesh. It was fear made manifest, and they quivered, crouched, and swooned. Like so many other humans, they waited to be eaten.

Except for Kuon.

"Rahhhhhhhhhhhhhhhhhhhhhhhhhhhhhhhhhhhhhhhhhhhhhhhhhhhh!"

Nobody realized that this scream had come from Okegawa Kuon. The instinctive need to kill Jave, which he acquired in his previous life, had reflexively pushed him into action. In the blink of an eye, he'd cut a mass dozens of times his size in half. He turned back to his classmates.

"Move!" His shout echoed through the room. His frozen classmates twitched. "Activate your DMs! Get the survivors to the maintenance bay!"

One of his classmates calmed down enough to ask, "Wh-what will you do?"

"Buy you some time."

"Wh-what about the injured?"

"Get their bubbles to activate and begin healing them, then carry them. If they don't have long, make sure they don't suffer."

"Y-you mean...kill them? We can't—"

There was another roar. It came from right next to them. A manta slammed into the windows. A massive body several meters long stabbed itself into the wall of the school, reaching tentacles through the broken windows and attacking. Kuon cut them all down and killed the manta clinging to the windows, shouting, "Do it now or you'll all die!"

His classmates started hastily picking up the wounded and carrying them out of the classroom. Outside, the hall and other classrooms were overrun with Jave. They had to cross the school-yard with no cover and reach the maintenance bay where the fighting would be particularly fierce. How many of them would make it? Kuon took a breath, hoping to increase that number even a little.

Nine-count Strike.

Kishin Ryuenbu, Mod.

Curved blue Blades sliced apart the Jave in the classrooms as well as the ones clinging to the windows. Kuon dove back into each classroom searching for Witch Bubbles or other signs of life in every corner of the school. There were no more Jave left, and he'd killed a lot of enemies, but...

"Argh...!" His chest hurt. His heart wasn't beating right. He was remotely operating magic Blades like Servants, so it was supposed to hurt a little, but this was rougher than he'd imagined.

It didn't carve away at his life like the ultimate art, but his master would definitely yell at him later.

A call came in on his comms. It was Fuji. "Was that Okegawa-kun? You're alive? Good. There are enemy main forces in the sky above us. Suzuka-kun is already headed for them. Regroup with her and annihilate them." His orders were terse, clipped, as if purged of all emotion.

Kuon was in no state to notice. "Aye aye, sir. Suzuka Hachishiki, heading to annihilate enemy forces."

Without realizing what he'd just said, Kuon shot upwards, glaring at the skies above. These foes had come not from the deep sea but from what lay right before his eyes: a Gate in the skies above Jogen Maneuver Academy.

Hanabi had gone into the Gate first, and was desperately battling the Queen. She didn't have the Kiryu with her, but she couldn't afford to hesitate. She had to kill this thing as soon as possible and get back to school to save more people. But alone...

"Servants!"

Wings flew out of her backpack, menacing the Queen. They shot down a number of enemy tentacles and bullets. The enemy fired back, but the Servants successfully dodged. Careful not to miss the warning signs of the hard-to-avoid tentacles-from-nowhere attacks, Hanabi readied her rifle.

Then a call came in from Fuji telling her Kuon would be there any moment. She felt strength surging into her. No matter how bad the situation, if he was there, they would find a way through it.

Just as she was down to one remaining Servant...

"Hanabi-senpai."

She heard Kuon's voice and turned towards him. But...

"Kuon...kun?"

As he came in the Gate, he looked like someone else. He seemed totally different. His voice flat, he asked, "Ready to go on Scout Nova Rifle max output?"

"Er, uh, of course."

"I'll hit it with a Reppakuzan. Crossfire. Put that Servant on me."

"Roger that."

There was no time to try and figure out what was bothering her about him. Hanabi sent her Servant to Kuon and waited for his signal. As he flew the other way, the Queen's bullets targeted him, too, but there were fewer coming her way as a result. That made it easier to get her rifle charged. "Ready," Kuon said. As he did...

Shichisei Kenbu: Mod. Tensetsu Shigure.

Time stopped. Her vision showed attack routes and the likely evasion routes the Queen would take, and Hanabi set her aim to one side of the enemy. Time resumed. In front and to the left of her, Kuon unleashed a sword of red light, passing to the Queen's side. Hanabi shot her rifle at her guts, a shot powerful enough to blow up a moon.

Screeeeeeeeeeeeeeeeeeeeeeeeeeeeeeeeeeeeeeeeeeeeeeeeeee!

Crossfire. Kuon's red light and Hanabi's white light hit it from both sides. Caught in the middle, the Queen had nowhere to go. Burned by terrifyingly high temperatures, she melted and evaporated, leaving no trace behind.

This was the first time they'd killed a Queen with anything but Kuon's ultimate art, but as Hanabi rushed to leave the Gate before it closed, she was less concerned with that than trying to figure out what it was that felt so off.

Since when does Kuon talk like that?

And his eyes. Like he was beaten down by everything, like...

Ahead of her, the extra-booster-covered back of Soukyu (Mod.) looked just like the Hero, back when he saved her during the fall of the capital.

Kuon and Hanabi returned to the school and began dispatching the remaining enemies.

Shortly afterwards, they found *her*.

Her right leg was melting.

The head of a light bullet had melted a lump of iron, and it was flowing like lava, eating into her skin, digging deeper and deeper. She'd gotten her DM activated so the fire that had burned her leg was out, but liquid metal was eating into her thigh through the Witch Bubble.

She was burning, her head in a daze. She tried to move her hands, but her body wouldn't listen to her. She couldn't move at all. But it was her body! This was weird. She managed to move her eyes and saw a dark red sky through the holes in the ceiling. There were desks and chairs and pieces of wall scattered all around her,

all on fire. There was someone lying next to her, but she couldn't move her head. *So hot melting, oh, someone, Hanabi, Okayama, Fuji, Kyuu-kun, anyone my leg, clean it off...*

Can't say that now. They're all really busy. We're lying here and the classmates who got their Maneuvers out in time are all desperately fighting off the monsters, yeah, like they're protecting us. Someone grabbed her left hand and yelled "Rin!" There was a whistling sound like a punctured lung, and it must be impossibly painful for them to talk, so why were they trying? She wanted to ask, but first they said...

"Look after...Jin for me..."

Who was Jin? She'd heard that name before. Who was it? After that she didn't hear anyone calling her name. Just the roars of the monsters and the screams and sobs of her classmates, ceaseless. The hand holding hers slid away, going limp. Her leg was still melting. *Won't someone please clean my leg? You can rub a high school girl's leg all you like for free, right now. Probably too late, though. Poor leg. Oh, I know Jin! Squad Leader Fuji. His name was Fuji Jindo, right? Then the one next to me is...*

Darkness.

Her eyes opened, and the ruined classroom ceiling was now a sterile white hospital ceiling.

"Unh..." Everything hurt. She moved her head. Sat up a little. And saw...

"Ah...ah..."

She knew it. The sheets on the right side down there were awfully flat.

"Ah...ahh...ahhh...ahhhhhhhhh..."

She'd thought as much. She covered her face with her hands. If only she could have moved them then.

Everything from Rin's right thigh on down was gone.

_//////////

The next day, they started cleaning the school.

People treated as "missing" were ones where they hadn't found a body; odds were high they'd been eaten during the fighting.

A hundred first-year students had entered junior high six months before. Of these, seventy-two were dead or missing, and twenty-eight were wounded.

Seventy percent of the Lunatic Order were MIA. The Fuji Squad was the only squad with all members still alive, but their sniper had lost a leg. Three members of the Sagara Squad, including the squad leader, were dead. One attacker, Okayama, had survived with injuries.

There was one more name Kuon was looking for. He scrolled mechanically down the list of the dead until he found her name.

Murakawa Squad, Control, Gotenba Nao.

Fuji was still picking a wedding dress, as if it hadn't hit him yet.

CHAPTER 3

Operation Jave World Annihilation

I T WAS ONE WEEK after the Jave attacked the school.

The Empire, the Alliance, and the human race had no time left, so Operation Jave World Annihilation was put in action. They would open a pseudo-Gate, send in Tooka's final weapon, and wipe out their enemy.

Accordingly, Jogen Maneuver Academy was disbanded and repurposed as the Imperial Air Force Jogen Base. Squad makeup and frame adjustments were proceeding at a feverish pitch. Their former headmaster, Nanahoshi Kaede, was appointed consultant/advisor and went to the Capital to secure frames. Tooka Nürburg was busy making adjustments to the final weapon and the Kiryu. After a mass funeral for their friends, the Fuji Squad was incorporated into the Air Force, with Kuon, Hanabi, and Fuji joining the operation. Rin, with her injuries, was on standby.

Scouts had confirmed a large number of Queens in Europe, incubating their eggs. The one country still holding their ground had finally fallen. On the Imperial mainland, Gate activity was

high, and the defenses in Fukuoka had proven inadequate; it was lost once more. Nanahoshi Kaede reported no changes in the capital yet, but that would not last forever.

After more than twenty years since they'd first appeared, the Jave were finally beginning their full-scale invasion. Mankind had been desperately struggling to survive against what had turned out to be merely their scouting parties.

To put it mildly, humanity was dangling on the edge of a cliff.

It was 8:58 AM, three hours before the operation was to begin. Hanabi was on the seventh floor of the Jogen 3ʳᵈ Municipal Hospital, visiting Rin.

This was hardly her first visit. When she heard Rin had lost a leg, Hanabi had felt like she'd lost her own. She couldn't even stand for a while. Rin's injuries were recovering well, but what she'd lost wasn't coming back.

It was my fault, Hanabi thought. She'd been right next to Rin when it happened. She should have helped her before heading to the Gate. How had she not noticed? If she'd just been paying a little more attention or waited for the DM diagnosis to run, she'd have known. Yet, no matter how many times she apologized, Rin insisted it wasn't her fault.

But it is my fault.

Alone together in a spacious private room, neither Hanabi nor Rin spoke. Every time Hanabi came to visit, she just sat with her head down while Rin stared out the window, saying nothing. They didn't know what to say to each other.

Eyes still on the window, Rin broke the silence. "You're deploying soon, Hanabi."

"...Mm."

"You okay? You're not bothering Kyuu-kun, are you?"

"No. Wait, I probably am."

"I know you are! You've been crying on his shoulders this whole time. You know, it's actually kind of a relief that I don't have to be your only sob pillow now?"

"Mm."

"Did...did you ask him about it?" Hanabi shook her head. Rin smiled faintly. "You're really feeble when it comes to that, huh?"

"But—"

"No, it's scary, I know. If I were in your shoes, I doubt I could ask."

"Mm..."

"Oh, I know!" Rin said, unconvincingly brightening up all of a sudden. "Yesterday, Okayama came by, even though I told him not to."

"Okayama-kun?" Hanabi looked up.

Rin gave her a sheepish smile. "He is *too* funny. You know what he said?"

"N-no idea..."

"He was all, 'I'll always protect you.' I went so red! He's such an idiot. I end up like this, but he still says he loves me. I've lost a leg! But he says he doesn't care. What an idiot. He should just forget about me."

"Don't talk like that!"

"Hanabi..." There was a sudden sob. "Don't you go anywhere, Hanabi." Rin's expression crumpled. "Nao...Nao's gone, but...I can't lose you, too." Tears started falling. "They took my leg away. They took Nao, and not just her. Sachikou and the Amakusa sisters and everyone else are gone! I'll never see them again, no matter how hard I look. No matter how long I wait, they'll never come back. There was so much I wanted to say to them. But I can never talk to them again."

"Rin...Rin...!"

"I miss them... I wanna see them again..." Still crying, Rin put her arms around Hanabi. Hanabi softly hugged her back. "So... Hanabi, promise me you won't die. Promise me you'll come back...!"

Hanabi remembered the first time she met Rin. The Hero had saved her, put her on an escape ship, and she'd found herself all alone at a Jogen refugee center until she was brought to the Motegi home. The head of the family heard what happened to her, grew sympathetic, and brought her into his home in the hopes that she'd be a friend to Rin, who was always lonely since her mother and father were too busy to pay much attention to her.

At first, Hanabi couldn't find it in herself to like Rin, and they fought a lot. Even then, all she had to do was stare hard enough, and Rin would always give in. Now she knew she'd been taking advantage of her sister. Rin always held her tight during her episodes. She even started taking lessons with her, lessons on things she'd hated doing and quit once before. She was nice. Hanabi was happy. She loved her. So Hanabi knew what to say.

"I promise! I promise I'll come back to you...!"

Goodbye, she said in her mind, bidding her sister farewell. Their embrace ended.

Rin gave her a sweet smile. "Good luck out there, Hanabi."

Hanabi left Rin's room, closed the door behind her, and didn't take another step. Lately, her thoughts kept looping around the same idea.

I can't be the Hero.

She couldn't be like Suzuka Hachishiki. She'd been trying desperately to be, had wanted to be like him ever since he'd saved her, but there was just no way.

She let far too many people die in Europe. She wasn't able to save her school or Nao or Rin. Command and the world at large acted like she was one of a heroic duo, but she didn't have the right. The word "Hero" was for people like Kuon. People who could go up against an impossible choice, pick "both," and actually pull it off, like he did.

She couldn't do that. Not only could she not pull it off, she couldn't even make the choice. She would just start crying and slump to the ground.

So Suzuka Hanabi wasn't a hero. Could never *be* a hero.

"The media are all talking about an idealized version of you, so of course the real you doesn't live up to it," her doctor said.

"You don't have to be a hero," Rin had told her.

She was done. She couldn't keep doing this. She didn't need to keep trying, and that thought made her feel so much better. *Oh,* she thought. *That's a weight off my chest.*

She gave up on her dream.

"Unh...hah...guh...enhhhhhh..."

The tears came streaming out of her. She felt so relieved, so much better, so why couldn't she stop crying? Leaning against the wall in the hospital corridor, Hanabi hid her face, ignoring the people passing by, not even trying to hide, just letting the sobs come.

_//////////⌐

It was 9:58 AM, two hours before the operation was to begin.

In the 1st Storage Bay of the Imperial Air Force Jogen Base—formerly Jogen Maneuver Academy—a girl stood in front of the completed new Kiryu model. Someone came up behind her and spoke.

"Tooka."

"...Onii-chan."

Okegawa Kuon and Tooka Nürburg. Brother and sister in a previous life, sharing what would almost certainly be their last conversation.

Tooka had called him here, and he'd made up his mind to act upbeat about it, since it was their last time together. He stood behind his sister, looking up at the massive frame. "You finished her new Kiryu, then." Tooka nodded. Kuon was impressed. *Even with the Core, getting it built in this short a time?* "You really are a genius," he said.

But she shook her head. "I'm not."

"What?"

"I'm not a genius. I just 'knew' everything from the very start."

"What do you mean?"

"The Crystal II, the Heavy Magic Engine; these were all things researched over there. I got those memories from the Mother."

"W-wait...'over there'? 'Mother'? What—" And then it dawned on him what that meant.

No.

"I remembered when I came in contact with them at Mid-Blue. I know who I am, where I came from, and why I'm here."

"Over there" was the Jave world. The "Mother" was a Jave Queen. Kuon didn't want to believe it, but Tooka said it anyway.

"I'm..." Suzuka Hachishiki's sister, eaten by the Jave, and reincarnated. "I was born from the Jave and dropped into this world."

It was unthinkable. The Queen who'd eaten Akigase Tooka thirty years before had made this fake thing, this monster, to resemble a human and investigate the world on this side. Tooka was half-human, half-Jave, a hybrid thing. Kuon nearly passed out.

"On the other side, there were people called Witches. They had powers that let them use magic without wearing a DM. But mankind used the Witches' power for war and transformed them into monsters known as Gévaudan."

Kuon didn't realize how similar that power was to the Eight Hidden Forms. He just listened in stunned silence.

"The humans only maintained control of the Witches for the first three years. Then the Witches attacked, killed, and consumed the humans. In no time at all, mankind was completely wiped out. That's why the Jave opened the Gate." Tooka went on.

"The Heavy Magic Engine works on the same principle as a Gate. That's how I could develop it. Fragments of the memories of the Queen who bore me were copied to my body."

"Copied..."

"That's why both my body and magic are the same as they were in my previous life. I was dropped into Nürburg without my memories, let free for a single purpose."

"And that is?"

"To find Okegawa Kuon."

"Me?"

"More accurately, to find Suzuka Hachishiki's new body. The one person on this side who stood a chance against the Jave. They knew the Gate had caused him to be reborn somewhere. That's why I was given memories telling me I was the heir to Shichisei Kenbu, like Suzuka Hachishiki had been. If I told people that, then you'd find me."

It seemed likely that at the end of his last life, when Hachishiki's soul had mingled with the Queen's, those memories had flowed into her. It was the same as how Kuon had known when the Queen would return.

Just as the enemy intended, Nanahoshi Kaede found Tooka. The rest, Kuon already knew. With no memories, Tooka discovered and developed Heavy Magic Technology, not knowing it was Jave technology, and eventually created an imitation Gate. She'd even secured the perfect position as Okegawa Kuon's sister. And now...

"The Academy was destroyed, and Europe fell...because of me,"

Tooka said. Tears streamed down her face. "When I opened that Gate, the soldiers that came out extracted data from me. Everything I learned over here is in their hands now. We're an open book. They knew what was going on in Europe, they knew where Suzuka Hachishiki's new body was, and they knew where the *nest* that threatened them was."

The school.

The school where Suzuka Hanabi and her Kiryu were, where Okegawa Kuon and the Shichisei Kenbu were, run by Nanahoshi Kaede, the strongest humanity had to offer, the biggest threat to the Jave the military had—Jogen Maneuver Academy.

"I'm sorry." Her expression never changed—perhaps that was the way she'd been made—but the tears flowed as Tooka apologized again. "I'm so sorry. This is all my fault. I'm so sorry. So many of your friends died, Squad Leader Fuji's fiancée died, Motegi Rin lost her leg, and it's all my fault."

Kuon couldn't say a word. He couldn't say anything to help her. It was all he could do to restrain the rage threatening to erupt within him. *No, not her,* Kuon thought, begging the part of him that was Suzuka Hachishiki for help. *Not her.*

Tooka sensed this struggle within him. "I wouldn't mind if you killed me right now. I know just how much Suzuka Hachishiki hates the Jave. I know he won't leave a single one of them alive. But...but...please wait until this operation is over." She paused. "I will destroy them and their world."

Even if it costs me my life, she thought. With that, Tooka turned and walked past him.

This was it. His last chance.

He could grab her shoulders; cut off her head.

Okegawa Kuon just stood there, unable to do either. His head was spinning. Hachishiki's soul was screaming for him to kill Tooka. Kuon was using all his magic and muscles to control it. *Not her, no. She's not one of them.*

How long did he stay like that? When he finally calmed down, Kuon checked the time on his Device. There was only an hour and a half left before the operation commenced. He still had time.

He turned to leave the storage bay...

"Kuon-kun."

And found Suzuka Hanabi standing there, a look of grim determination on her face.

_//////////

Earlier...

Tooka had told Hanabi she wanted to talk, so she'd managed to get herself to the storage bay somehow, wiping the tears that just wouldn't stop. She'd overheard everything from just outside.

Hanabi knew Tooka had deliberately let her hear. What she said made the world spin around Hanabi. She had to lean against the wall for support, struggling to keep herself from hyperventilating.

Why?

After a while, Tooka stopped talking to Kuon and went over

to Hanabi. Her face was expressionless, so much so that it made alarm clocks look more approachable. Then, like before, Tooka bowed her head. "I'm the one who hurt your sister—Rin-san."

That's not true, Hanabi thought. But she couldn't speak. She was sure she'd lash out.

Head still bowed, Tooka spoke flatly. "I have memories of my previous life. I was onii-chan's little sister. But in that life, we never lived together. In this life, too, I'm unable to stay with him, no matter how much I want to."

Her expression never changed, her voice devoid of emotion, so why were the tears rolling down her cheeks so convincing?

Tooka really, genuinely didn't want to leave Kuon behind. She hated the idea so much it left her in tears.

Hanabi understood that so much it hurt. She felt the same way.

"But don't worry," Tooka reassured her. "When onii-chan is with you, he always looks happy. Hanabi-onee-sama, if you're with him, I believe the odds of him having a happy life improve."

"I..."

"Please look after him." Tooka bowed like a machine and went away.

Why? Hanabi thought. This was all too much. Her head was spinning. She had to make up her mind. Had to make a decision. Had to steel herself.

Tooka had left him in her hands and told her to look after him. But if she didn't hear the truth from him, she could never truly trust him.

"Kuon-kun."

At the sound of his name, Kuon turned and saw Hanabi.

Her eyes were swollen from crying, clearly beside herself. She wasn't at all ready for this operation. Kuon didn't blame her. They were all on the brink. "Hanabi-senpai. Don't worry. This operation will end everything," he said, trying to encourage her.

But she just said, "Kuon-kun..." again. Then she asked, "Is it true you have memories of your previous life like Tooka-chan does?"

She finally asked, he thought. But he hadn't expected it now. He took a breath and then let it out. "Yes."

Hanabi's shoulders shook, sobbing. "Then, you were..." She tilted her head down, not looking at him. "You were the Hero?"

He'd kept that to himself all this time. The least he could do was be honest now. "Yes."

"That can't be true."

"It's true."

"It can't be. I mean..."

"I was Suzuka Hachishiki. I remember everything."

"Don't—"

"I remember saving you thirteen years ago. I remember dying shortly after. Everything."

"Why?" she whispered. "Why didn't you say so? Why didn't you tell me? When we first met, when we first started working together...that night. This is too cruel, Kuon-kun. Too awful."

"I'm really sorry. Master told me not to—"

"The headmaster? That's why you didn't say anything?" she said, her voice raised in anger.

"N-no, not just—"

"You knew how much I admired *you!* You knew how much I admired *him!*"

"...Yeah."

"But you didn't trust me with this?"

"That's not...this was my—"

When Kuon spluttered, Hanabi cut him off, crying. "I mean, I mean, you didn't say the thing that matters most...!"

She was right. Kuon hadn't told her. That he'd been told not to was just a cowardly excuse. He'd simply been afraid to tell her. He was afraid it would disillusion her, afraid she would push him away. He'd just wanted to avoid getting hurt, and this was the result. He'd made her cry instead.

She was crying because of him.

"You didn't tell me anything... You kept it all from me. There was so much I wanted to talk about, but...I always wanted to tell you...to thank you for saving me. I never thanked you properly... so why...why..." Hanabi buried her face in her hands. "Why did you only show yourself to me now?" Her voice was strangled, like it was forcing its way out of her. "I already know I can never be like you...!" Her legs buckled out from under her, and she fell to the floor of the storage bay.

"Senpai," he said, about to touch her shoulder.

"I'm sorry. I can do this. I'll do it right. I won't sully your name.

I'll be fine..." She brushed his hand away, muttering, eyes fixed on the cold floor.

"Senpai...?"

"I've always looked up to you. I wanted to be like you...but I can't be. I've given up. But if you're here now..." She looked up at Kuon—at Hachishiki. The Bushi Hime got to her feet. "We will win."

"Um, Senpai...? Are you okay...?"

"Sorry... No, that's not right. Mm, yes. I know. I lost control for a moment there, Kuon-kun. Or should I call you Hero?"

It hurt to see her fake it like this.

To become a hero, Hanabi had unconsciously divided herself into two people, the weaker Maiden and the stronger Bushi. She was forcing herself into the latter role now because that was the only way she could stand upright.

"No, Kuon's better...but..."

"Right, okay. I'll go on ahead. See you later." She turned on her heel and walked away. Kuon was left staring blankly after her, unable to say a word.

_//////////┌

It was 11:45 AM, fifteen minutes before the operation was to begin. Nearly all forces the alliance and Empire had were assembled in Mid-Blue airspace near Aohime Island. Preparations for the operation were nearly complete. The "mirror" was set up, and the Nürburg, with Tooka on board, was in position.

The flagship *Kuou* was surrounded by an intimidating number of motherships. From there, the fleet commander Admiral Shirota addressed all assembled. He was a grizzled veteran. His hair was turning white, but years in the field had kept him in prime physical shape with no signs of deterioration. The conscience of high command, he'd furiously argued both publicly and privately against the decision to send the Student Echelon alone into the pseudo-Gate last time. He was the kind of macho grandpa who'd earned the trust of his wife, HQ, and the fiercest Air Force Cavalleria.

"The goal of this operation is to send the Nürburg to the Jave's world and destroy their solar system. The fate of the Empire and the human race will be decided here!" Shirota said.

Tooka and the mechanics had barely slept the last week getting things ready. As a result, they'd finished in time for the operation—the product of sheer desperation. All that remained were the final checks, and those would be completed in the next fifteen minutes, at which point they'd open another pseudo-Gate.

Kuon was waiting in the storage bay of a mobile mothership at 30,000 meters, along with Hanabi and her Kiryu. Hanabi only managed to deploy her Maneuver after a military doctor had given her some simple hypnosis and a few drugs to calm her down. Before that, she had been unable to use a DM at all.

Fuji joined them, his Division Maneuver already active. Surprised, Kuon asked, "You're good already, Squad Leader?"

After his fiancée's death, Fuji went on leave until right before the operation. He'd gone to visit Nao's family for the wake. "Yeah,

sorry, Okegawa-kun. The time for grieving's over. Now it's time to avenge Nao and the others."

Fuji looked just like he always did, so Kuon nodded. "Yeah. Let's win this thing."

Hanabi was already docked with the Kiryu, so she popped open a window. "You came, Fuji-kun?"

She sounded cold, and Fuji picked up on it immediately. "Sorry I've troubled you. And thanks."

"That goes for all of us. Don't worry about it." Then she whispered, "Either way, it ends today."

The Fuji Squad and the majority of the other squads were deployed on the far side of the mirror. When the Nürburg opened the Gate and the enemy came flooding out, they'd be ready for them. They'd laid traps for them. A terrifying number of hover mines were scattered everywhere, enough to darken the sky. When the pseudo-Gate opened, the enemies would charge headlong into that minefield. The ensuing fireworks would be the signal for the Fuji Squad's Kiryu to drop a bomb from above, buying time for the Nürburg to enter the pseudo-Gate. It would then open a door on the other side and enter the Jave world. Tooka would eject, the Nürburg would blow itself up, and the Jave solar system would collapse into a magical black hole.

That was command's plan, anyway.

But the best laid plans often go awry, especially when those plans have the fate of the human race at stake.

Admiral Shirota's speech was still in progress. "May you all fight well," he said.

And then the sky split open.

"Multiple Heavy Magic Reactions near the Pseudo-Gate!"

"What?! The operation hasn't begun!"

"These are...enemy Gates! Four...no, five! Five Gates!"

"Jesus!"

"The Gates are opening!"

Black fields appeared above and around the mirror. Crackling, sparks flying, five Jave Gates yawned open.

Manta came flying out in the opposite direction from the last fight, headed right towards the Nürburg. In other words, the minefield was useless, and the troops were positioned in the worst possible place.

Admirable Shirota was flooded with reports from his staff.

"They've avoided the minefield!"

"Enemy mantas swarming the Nürburg!"

"Commence operation!" Shirota yelled. "Get that pseudo-Gate open!"

"But the final checks..."

"Forget them! They'll destroy the Nürburg! We'll be too late!"

"Roger that!"

A moment later, dozens of mantas penetrated the Heavy Magic Field surrounding the Nürburg.

The operation had begun.

The Air Force units began attacking the Jave clustered on the far side of the pseudo-Gate. The attackers dove in, the snipers

backed them up, and the enemy didn't budge. After all, there were five Gates with five times the number of enemies in most battles. And if there were Gates...

"Enemy Queens! Five of them!"

"Damn it, they're already arriving?!"

Queens to the side of the Nürburg were slowly emerging from the five black moons around the pseudo-Gate. Cavalleria fighting the manta nearby were quickly snagged by their tentacles and hurled into countless mouths, eaten alive in passing.

"Arghhhhh!"

"No, noooo!"

"Damn iiiiit!"

Cavalleria screams echoed. In their midst, the Queens' conical bodies turned towards the sky, gathering light.

"Evasive actions!" Admiral Shirota yelled. "All ships, move to—"

Bam bam bam bam bam! Five massive white lights flashed. The mobile motherships ringing the *Kuou* exploded one after the other, going up in flames, and a number of them fell to the ocean below. Half the forty ships in the fleet were lost in an instant, and the Queens were charging another round.

"Second barrage, incoming!"

"Don't let them fire!"

"Too late, interference can't make it in time!"

The lights grew larger. Then...

"Roger, counterattacking."

Two even larger bullets swallowed up one of the Queens,

detonating it. Those bullets were High Nova Launcher shots, which meant...

"The Kiryu! You made it in time!"

It took time to get the Heavy Magic Engine for their newest weapon running, and the battle had started unexpectedly, so the Kiryu had only just dropped down. It fired another round before the Queens could react.

"Twin Nova Launcher, firing," the Bushi Hime whispered calmly. As she did, two bullets fired at once. The targeted Queen tried to flee to the side but wasn't fast enough. A direct hit vaporized her. The two bullets didn't overlap but left a gap between them, preventing the enemy's escape.

The three remaining Queens fired back, but the Kiryu made no attempt to dodge, flying straight at their bullets and meeting them head on. With the Heavy Magic Field at maximum output, the enemy bullets easily slid off it, and the Kiryu's twin heads opened, howling.

Screeeeeeeeeeeeeeeeeeeeeeeeeeeeeeeeeeeeeeeeeee...!

A Queen howled as it was bathed in light bullets, dissolving as the Kiryu swooped by. The two-headed dragon flew between the pseudo-Gate and the ocean surface, turned 180 degrees, and targeted the two remaining Queens.

The rider spoke. "Reimei (Second Drag Ride), exterminating opposition."

Tooka Nürburg had used the recovered Kiryu Core to make a new mechanical dragon, the Second Drag Ride. Wearing it was one of the Twin Star Heroes—the Division 5, Suzuka Hanabi.

Kuon and Fuji rode tandem on her back, both for protection and for backup.

The Queens moved.

Screeeeeeeeeeeee!

The mantas attacking the Air Force wheeled back, charging the Kiryu, in a Jave assault designed to smash through the Heavy Magic Field.

"Hmph," Hanabi snorted, sounding bored. She launched weapon containers from both the Kiryu's wings. Hundreds of Servants flew out, firing a torrent of light bullets that easily halted the wave of trash Jave. Before that torrent died down, she fired her main weapon.

Bwam!

Piercing through the Jave's red mist and shock waves, the two bullets passed below the pseudo-Gate, swallowing a Queen. Her death throes echoed. Mankind's mortal enemy, so threatening a moment before, vanished without a trace.

That was easy, thought Hanabi. She could tell she was strangely unemotional. Maybe it was the shock of forcing her personality change, or the influence of the hypnotism. To protect the fragile screams of her psyche, she was processing everything like it was taking place far away, somewhere with no connection to her. There was a lid on her emotions.

So perhaps what happened next didn't even count as letting her guard down.

"Suzuka-kun!"

The cry from her squad leader barely registered. *What's he all*

worked up about? she thought. *The enemy attacks can't affect them, and the last one isn't even facing us.*

Isn't facing us?

It took her two full seconds to realize that was strange.

A fatal two seconds.

"Nürburg, major damage!"

"What?!"

The flagship crew and admiral's screams echoed in her ears. On the other side of the pseudo-Gate, in the shadow of her minions' desperate cover, the last Queen's bulk was wrapped around the Nürburg. Countless tentacles writhed around it. For two full seconds, Hanabi stared blankly as the Queen squeezed.

She couldn't do anything.

The mirror split. Cracks ran across its surface right before it shattered. On the *Kuou*'s bridge, they watched, helpless to do anything.

"Pseudo-Gate has collapsed! Nürburg's Gate functions ceasing. Admiral!"

"Has the operation failed?"

"Wait..."

"Now what?"

"No! Nürburg moving! Entering enemy Gate!"

"That fool!" Shirota roared. He opened a comm immediately. "Don't, Tooka-kun! The enemy Gate isn't stable! We can't maintain it! You'll never make it back!"

"Doesn't matter," Tooka replied.

"It does! Wait till we repair your machine!"

"More enemy Gates will open before that happens. Next time it'll be more than five. This time they will wipe us out."

"But—"

"This is my decision, Admiral. You know the truth about the Nürburg, and you still gave me this opportunity, for which I am grateful."

"Tooka-kun, don't!"

The massive black egg changed course. With the last Queen still clinging to it, it dove into the enemy's Gate, and there...

"Tooka!"

Kuon came racing after her, leaving the Kiryu behind. He remembered what Tooka had said: *I'm so sorry. This is all my fault.*

Why couldn't he just have said, "It isn't"?

He could have told her, "This was all the Jave's doing. You didn't know. You were just used. You were eaten, killed. It isn't your fault. You did nothing wrong."

Why hadn't he just said that?

The Nürburg was entirely inside the enemy Gate. Tooka opened a private comm to Kuon. "Goodbye, onii-chan. I'm going back to the world where I was born."

"No, wait!"

"I'm glad we could be together, even if only for a little while."

Those were parting words. A wave of anger he couldn't understand coursed through Kuon's entire body. Tooka was prepared to sacrifice her life to save the world. Once again, a member of his family was about to die right before his eyes at the hands of the Jave.

Suzuka Hachishiki's sister.

His sister.

Just like his father and mother and the nuns and his friends at the orphanage and his friends in the Air Force. He couldn't let that happen. "You hideous mutant monsters...!"

Did the Jave Queen hear *him* whisper? Or sense something else? The Queen clinging to the Nürburg turned, reaching her tentacles towards Kuon as he approached.

"Outta my way!"

Dodging with Tensetsu, he took the Shitotsu stance...

Screeeeeeeeeeeeeeeeeeeeeeeescccrrrrreeeeeeeeeeeeeeeeeee!

The Queen's light of life scattered, turning to mist. Without hesitation, he'd unleashed the ultimate art he'd been forbidden to use.

Kuon went silent.

And then *he* went after Tooka and was about to enter the collapsing Gate when...

"Kuon-kun!"

Hanabi came after him. Fuji wasn't with her, so she must have cut him loose. She was trying to use the Kiryu's Heavy Magic Engines to maintain the Gate. "The Gate's closing!" she yelled, grabbing Kuon's arm. "It'll collapse before you can catch Tooka-chan!"

"Let go of me."

"You won't make it in time!"

"Let. Go." Kuon brushed her arm off him. As he did so, the Kiryu's engine stalled again.

"No...why...?" Hanabi cried.

"You're going to live," said the other half of the Twin Star Heroes—no, the man once called the Hero. He turned back to look at Hanabi. "I've got to go avenge everyone."

She'd heard those words before. Hearing them again now stopped her, like she'd frozen up. *This is my fault,* Hanabi thought. *If only I'd realized what the Queen was doing faster. If I'd just killed them all without letting them do anything.*

Kuon wouldn't have turned back into *him.*

In front of her was the Hero who'd died thirteen years ago. Once again, he was going to leave her behind and head into a Gate.

While she reeled, Kuon turned his back on her and went inside the closing Gate. With the Kiryu's engine stalled, she couldn't go after him. Fuji called her name, and at last she resumed functioning.

"Wait, don't go! Hero!" She reached out, shouting, but it didn't reach him. The Gate swallowed Kuon, closing in front of her. He never once looked back.

"Why...?"

The Kiryu was falling. It faced the sky as gravity dragged her towards the ocean. Before her eyes, the black moon with the Soukyu inside vanished completely.

"No...no..."

Her hands reached out towards the sky, and then she covered her face with them.

"Whyy....?!"

She hit the water. The Reimei's bubble protected her, and as she sank below the surface, she let out a wail that no one heard.

"Whyyyyyy....?!"

She'd been left behind again. He hadn't chosen her.

She was alone once more.

_//////////⌐

There was a rainbow flowing past Tooka.

It felt like tumbling into a valley or climbing a sheer cliff face, like both and neither at the same time. The wall was covered in a pattern of light in all colors of the rainbow, and it flowed past her like a river or a waterfall. Each part of the flow was a "time" and a "world", and in the cockpit of her giant cracked egg, Tooka Nürburg was certain of one thing.

She was crossing over multiple axes in time, across multiple lines between worlds, on her way to the Jave world.

She was inside the Gate. The door on the other side was open, and she was on her way through. In a sense, that was home—where her current body was born. Akigase Tooka had been eaten, and the mother that had caused her to be reborn as Tooka Nürburg was on that side.

Maybe...

Maybe that side was a world of beauty. There were no humans. Perhaps it was filled with primordial forests. Then the rainbow abruptly ended, and she was through the Gate.

At least, she should have been. But this didn't make sense.

The landscape before her was exactly like the capital.

The images shown on her cockpit's screens showed the ruins of a city, as if people had been living there until quite recently. There were reddish-black conical shapes like Jave eggs around, but this world didn't seem like their nest. However, Tooka's memories said otherwise. She knew this was another Earth, a parallel world to the one Kuon and his friends lived on.

The area around the Capital was unnaturally dark, but she could see sunlight in the distance. She looked up to find the reason. The sky was covered by a massive disc-shaped Jave floating overhead with a terrifying number of mouths and eyes staring at Tooka and the Nürburg.

I have to do this.

Before the enemy attacked her, while it was still just watching, she needed to activate the magic black hole and destroy this solar system.

She booted the program. Heavy Magic Engines were at full power. The field was active, disseminating the energy from the Crystal II. She would open two Gates inside it, and they'd expand until a black hole large enough to swallow—

Screeeeeeeeeeeeeeeeeeeeeeeeessssccccccccrreeeeaaaaaaaaaaaaaaaaaaaaa aaaaaaaaaaaaaaaaaaaaaaaaaaaaaaaaaaaaaaaaaaaaaaaaaaaaaaaaaaaaaaaaaa aaaaaaaaaaaaaaaaaaaaaaaaaaaaaaaaaaaaaaaaaaaaaaaaaaaaaaaaaaaaaaaaaa aaaaaaaaaaaaaaaaaaaaaaaaaaaaaaaaaaaaaaaaaaiiiiiiiiiiiiiiiiiiiiiiiiiii iiiiiiiiiiiiiiiiiiiiiiiieeeeeeeeeeeeeeeeeeeeeeeeeeeeeeeeeeeeeeeeeeeee!

It shook her entire body. It took ages for her to realize the shock wave her sensors picked up was a *sound*.

It required even more processing before she knew this was the voice of the Jave covering the sky. It was a war cry, the brutal scream of a carnivore who'd spotted prey and was summoning its pack.

Like a swarm of locusts, black shadows closed in on the Nürburg from all directions. Every one of those was a manta-type Jave, and with this machine using its Heavy Magic Field to generate a black hole Gate, it would never stand a chance.

She was about to die.

Somehow, she found herself crying. She was supposed to be half-Jave, yet she was afraid to die. But her hands never stopped advancing the program. She'd removed the last safety device, and all she had left to do was pull the trigger. If she did, the Nürburg would become multiple Gates, swallow the Jave nest, and vanish. And she would be the first to die.

She hesitated for a tiny moment. She closed her eyes.

The face she pictured was the master who'd essentially raised her. The mother who'd taken in a total stranger, a fraud pretending to be the heir to her precious Fencing school, and raised her like her own daughter. Nanahoshi Kaede was strong, kind, and cool. Tooka loved her.

Mother, thank you for everything. And goodbye.

She pulled the trigger.

The next moment felt endless. She forgot to breathe. A single second seemed to take hours. She felt faint. A tear fell from Tooka's face, falling slowly like a feather. The tear hit the floor of the cockpit, and smaller droplets splattered around it, and she felt like she'd been watching it fall for a full day.

But nothing happened.

"Huh...?"

She pulled the trigger again. No change. Her eyes swept across the monitors around her. Engine good, field out, oil and electric gauges normal, subsystems all clear...except one.

Magic Pressure was at 99.98%.

So close. The magic pressure required to generate the first Gate wasn't functioning because of the damage it took when the Queen attacked her back on Earth.

No!

The mantas were almost here. She hurriedly expanded her Heavy Magic Field. She had to buy herself enough time to repair the machine. The high capacity field barely withstood the enemy assault. The mantas stopped, as if stabbed into the Nürburg's field. She had approximately eight seconds before they broke through. That much time to repair the—

A massive hand reached down from the sky, a tentacle from the disc Jave. Its tip touched the field around the Nürburg and pulsed, sending ripples across the surface of the field.

Vorp.

"Unghhh....?!"

It felt like something stirring her brain. A scream tore out of her. Electricity ran from her brain down to her tailbone, and her back arched itself. She was inside the cockpit, but the disc Jave had created a magical link to her.

"Augh...ghhh, ah, no, st-stoppp, eek, ahhhhhhhhhhhhhh!"

It was kneading the inside of her head. Her vision warped,

twisted, flipped. Waves of pain ran across her body as though her skin were being peeled. Her body convulsed like every fluid in it was flowing backwards, and she was not even allowed to pass out, only scream and cry. *Forgive me. Save me. Kill me.* Those three wishes came out as screams, and even as they did, she knew what it was they were after.

Okegawa Kuon floated across the back of her mind.

The Jave contact was pulling up his memories.

Onii...cha—

Tooka was just happy she'd remembered him before she died. She was even grateful to the Jave for it. It saved her. Now she could die in peace. She closed her eyes.

Shichisei Kenbu.

Just then, she heard a familiar voice and was released from all pain. On the screens, she saw the manta around the Nürburg and the disc Jave's tentacle sliced to pieces by a blue Blade. Before she could process what that meant, Tooka passed out.

Wrapped in a black cloak, a single Cavalleria swept out of the Gate behind the Nürburg just before it vanished. Running sideways across the sky, he fired the boosters that lined his cloak and jumped. "Jumped" was definitely more accurate than "flew." He might not be able to move freely through the air, but he could launch himself. He landed on one knee on empty space a few centimeters above the Nürburg's Heavy Magic Field and rose to his feet.

"The Black Hole Gate hasn't been activated. She failed?"

It was Okegawa Kuon, wearing Soukyu (Pleiades Wind) and sporting a new extra weapon Tooka had made specifically for him. One he hadn't had a chance to use while serving as the Kiryu's backup.

Tooka's not responding. She's alive, but...

He wanted to get inside the Nürburg and slap her awake, but he didn't have time. He'd used Ryuenbu to slash away all the enemies around them, but reinforcements would be coming quickly. Most of all...

"Don't you look down at me, monster," Kuon muttered, glaring at the massive disc-shaped Jave floating above him. He'd never seen this type before, and it seemed likely this one even out-ranked the Queens. If he couldn't kill it, they'd never get a black hole Gate open, even if Tooka did wake up. The soul of Suzuka Hachishiki that had awakened within Kuon forced his face into a grin. The fury of a hero whose parents and family and friends and sister had all been murdered was tainting Kuon's own heart. Kuon had seen his friends and school and the people he'd tried to save in Europe slaughtered in the same way, and found it intensely satisfying to let himself bathe in the flames of that fury.

"Perfect. You'll be the ideal test for my new form."

He pulled the Ultra Magic Hardened Blade from his hip. The thruster nozzles inside his cloak lifted him up. A horrific quantity of eyes stared down at him from the disc above. He took a breath.

"Let's go, Pleiades Wind!"

The disc Jave fired several hundred light bullets, and Kuon vanished.

As the invisible bullets slid off the Nürburg's field and slammed into the ground, Kuon appeared diagonally above where he'd been. He hung there for a moment and then kicked off the air, leaping again. Cloak fluttering, he shot upwards towards the enemy looming far above.

Pleiades Wind was a hell of a thing Tooka had created for the Gate extermination operation. It kept the Shichisei Kenbu's Nine-count Strike intact but took the bulky, cumbersome additional boosters, minimized them, and lined his cloak with them. The cloak itself was a cooling system for the thruster nozzles.

It also had one more feature.

"This is perfect, Tooka," Kuon grinned, having stair-jumped all the way above the disc Jave. The cloaks thrusters were capable of momentary bursts of power, enabling large jumps but not the continuous output of your average DM. Division 1 power simply wasn't suited for aerial combat.

But this gave Kuon the means to overcome that weakness.

He paused again in mid-air. At his feet was a round space approximately three meters wide. In that one place, the color of the sky and the flow of the clouds changed. Light reflected off of it like a round mirror.

Kuon was standing on a transparent, glass-like disc. The blue of the sky and the flow of the clouds and the light of the sun were all reflected off this virtual image. This was the Pleiades Wind's secondary function, the Hortensie Felt—a function that generated an invisible foothold in mid-air.

The principle was simple: a portion of the Witch Bubble that normally surrounded him was instead solidified at his feet. This had been a common function in the first-generation DMs, but as time went on, the focus shifted to aerial combat using high-level magic. Since generating the foothold minimized the energy directed to the Witch Bubble and left the Cavalleria nearly defenseless, the technology was soon deprecated and eventually forgotten entirely. Tooka had happened across it in a German museum, displayed like a relic of ancient times. But for someone with magic as low as Kuon's, a foothold was huge help.

The Witch Bubble was a magical weapon from the previous century, allowing operation in outer space or the ocean depths alike. It was an invincible shield of magic impenetrable by any physical attack, whether it be a nuclear missile or an orbital strike. Kuon was moving faster than the speed of sound, but the impact of his landing would never shatter it, which was ideal.

It was a Witch Wall that could not be harmed except by Jave attacks, since both their flesh and bullets were made of magic.

Countless eyes on the top of the disc Jave turned towards him. By then, a hail of light bullets had already shattered his foothold. The remains of it reverted to invisible particles, pulled after Kuon—who had leapt away a few moments ago—like iron filings drawn to a magnet.

Kuon made a foothold directly above it. He landed on it upside down and spread his cloak.

Shichisei Kenbu.

Bam! An ear-splitting crack echoed as the Cavalleria easily

broke through the sound barrier, lunging towards the disc Jave. With the Jave's aim thrown off, Kuon didn't even need to dodge its bullets; they passed harmlessly by. It gathered several hundred tentacles in an attempt to block his path, but...

Chijin.

He was suddenly somewhere else—at the edge of the disc. This art combined his shukuchi with the thruster's output. His left arm thrust forward, heedless of his master's warnings.

Ultimate Art: Mumyo Tosen.

The Blade in Kuon's hand shot forward. It struck the light of life he saw within the disc Jave, generating Magical Dispersal.

Screeeeeeeeeeeeeeeee!

As the disc Jave fired bullets in Kuon's direction, more tentacles burned away the area Kuon had stabbed. The disc was cutting a portion of its own flesh away, like amputating a gangrened limb.

"...Tch."

Kuon frowned as he leapt wildly through the air, struggling to calm his ragged heartbeat. Was this why he'd seen several lights of life? Was this thing not a single Jave but several fused together? He couldn't see a brain or any sort of command center. He supposed that meant he'd just have to kill all of them.

"Nine-count Strike."

As Kuon bounded around, nine arms fanned out from the outside of the cloak on his back. With this halo backing him, Kuon swung his Blade sideways, focusing his magic.

"Shijin—Reppakuzan!"

A massive, seemingly infinite red light flew towards the disc

Jave. It threw up hundreds of glowing tentacles, blocking Kuon's red sword with a crackle that shook the air. Two seconds later, the Reppakuzan's power weakened and the sword dispersed, the particles scattering through the air. One side of the disc had melted a little, but he'd been unable to significantly damage the disc Jave.

"Damn it...!"

Nine-count Strike allowed him to boost his magic to Division 5 for a mere nine seconds. He'd used six of those seconds and barely scratched it. While back on his foothold, he tried to catch his breath and accept that fact.

The disc Jave fired bullets in Kuon's direction. He used Tensetsu to predict the future, searching for evasion routes, and saw a surprising attack line. There weren't just lines in front of him but also an insane number of them coming from below. Retreating, he dodged them all, and then he spied the source.

A few dozen Queens were gathering on the surface.

"...Tch."

The click of his tongue was inaudible over the roar of the enemy attacks, even to him. Light bullets fired at him in such huge quantities that it was barely even a metaphor for rain anymore. He dodged with a bound, knocking them aside with his twin Blades, but he couldn't keep that up forever. Even using shukuchi to rapidly move around, even using Tensetsu to predict the future, there was nothing he could do if there was nowhere to dodge to. He fled higher and higher, and the enemy followed. Kuon spied a swarm of mantas through the bullets and quickly swung a Blade, but he never saw the other group coming from his blind spot.

With time frozen by Tensetsu, he saw gnashing teeth behind and below him, realizing there was no way to dodge.

Don't screw this up, he told himself. *If you make the wrong move, you're dead.* Kuon spent what felt like fifteen full seconds staring at the inevitable future a second ahead. Before Tensetsu ran out, he made his choice.

Not to die, though. This wasn't the time for that.

No, he'd made up his mind to leave one of them behind.

A manta whooshed by on his right. Kuon threw himself left, avoiding instant death. A burning heat ran through his right arm. The Witch Bubble quickly stopped the bleeding, covering his arm in bubble-like light.

Everything below his right elbow had been eaten.

"Shit! That really hurt, asshole...!"

The pain and shock left him dizzy, but he didn't have time to cry about it. Watching the manta fly off as it chewed his arm, Kuon turned and braced himself. The rain of bullets had died down, but the Queens had started producing a flood of mantas. Kuon laughed out loud. Alone like this, they were giving him a real run for his money.

All I need is one arm, Kuon thought. *I can still use my ultimate art.* He was going to die here anyway, so no point worrying about the consequences. Let it chip his life away.

As he'd run, he'd been climbing; now he was at 20,000 meters. The former Hero glared down, letting hatred burn within.

"Come at me."

His eyes no longer saw the present. He was seeing distant

memories, monsters swarming over towns that had burned just like this one. There was someone he loved, but he'd forgotten who.

He couldn't afford to remember.

Nearly three days had passed since Kuon and Tooka vanished through the Gate.

There were no reports of Gates vanishing anywhere in the world or any signs that a Heavy Magic Collapse had been triggered. The Empire and the Alliance concluded that Tooka had failed.

Humanity had only one hope remaining: use the Heavy Magic Engine on the Kiryu to force open a Gate, locate the Nürburg where it lay on the other side, and this time generate a magic black hole. It was their only chance.

But they had no way of knowing if the Nürburg was intact. No way of knowing the situation beyond the Gate. Comms couldn't go through. All they knew was that no further Gates had opened.

The biggest impediment to their plan was that the only person who could fly the Kiryu, Suzuka Hanabi, had yet to recover from that battle. She was the sole Division 5 remaining.

Rin had chosen crutches over a wheelchair. She'd come running from her own hospital, moving through the ship on her remaining leg and the crutches. The sensation that her missing leg was still there was a trick of the mind, but she had phantom pains from everything below the thigh.

Medication hadn't been enough for Hanabi. Therapy wasn't helping her, either. Squad Leader Fuji had called Rin to the *Kuou*'s medical bay, saying that Hanabi needed Rin's voice. So dumb. Her voice wasn't magic. If she could help at all, it would be some other way.

Hanabi.

She thought about slapping her and dragging her along, no matter how much she cried and wailed. Just grabbing her by the scruff of her neck and pulling her out. She was certain this was her duty as her friend and adopted sister.

But this resolve died the moment she saw Hanabi's face.

"She thought she was five years old until yesterday," a nurse whispered.

Yeah, Rin thought. The situation was far too similar.

The girl here had lost the will to live. Rin's sister lay there, expressionless, tears flowing without end. No trace of the Bushi Hime or any kind of hero remaining. Rin felt like murdering anyone who'd try and make this girl fight again.

Then I suppose the first thing I oughta do is kill myself, Rin thought, laughing to herself.

She had to say it. If she didn't, they were all dead.

"Hanabi..." Saying the rest of it felt so much harder than just dying. If only it were just her who would die here. She took a deep breath and finished the sentence. "Get up. Open the Gate. Fight for us."

Hanabi looked at Rin as if she'd given up on everything. Ignoring the unspoken plea, Rin glared back at her, confident she

was doing the cruelest possible thing. "You can't be weak now. Got it? If you don't fight, we all die. When this is done, feel free to come kill me. But first, you've got to go kill those monsters."

Trembling, Hanabi shook her head. "I can't... I can't do it anymore..."

"You can. Hanabi, you can do it. I know you better than anyone, and I say you can do it. Trust me. You've got this. I promise. Open that Gate, save Kyuu-kun and Tooka-chan, and blow their world to hell. See? Easy."

"Then...then why don't you—" Hanabi stopped herself. Clearly she'd been about to suggest that Rin do it.

"I can't do it, Hanabi. I'm not Division 5. I know you never asked to be that strong. But you chose to be a Cavalleria because you wanted to be like the Hero, right?"

"But...but..."

Rin tried a new tactic. "Don't you want to save Kyuu-kun?"

"I...!"

"Yeah, it sucks he didn't tell you about his past life. One thing to keep that from us, total dick move to keep it from you. But you still love him, right?"

Hanabi said nothing.

"Otherwise, you wouldn't be this upset just because he left you behind. Clearly, at the end, his mind was Suzuka Hachishiki's again. 'Cause he's a huge idiot. Anyone who'd drop the girl they love to go avenge some crap from their past life is definitely the dumbest idiot who ever lived. You with me there, Hanabi?"

Hanabi still said nothing.

"Of course, if the girl that idiot dropped is gonna be all sad like this, you're almost as dumb as he is. And the fact that our lives are in the hands of this pair of nitwits is the dumbest thing about this!"

Even now, Hanabi said nothing. But Rin could see her grip on the sheets getting tighter. "Tell me, Hanabi," she said. "Why do you think Okegawa Kuon doesn't need you?"

Hanabi's lips moved wordlessly, but instead of sound, tears started flowing. Sobbing, she finally said, "He... He didn't tell me about his past life...he left me behind..."

Hmph, Rin thought. *But...* "He didn't tell you because he's a nitwit, and he left you behind so you'd survive. Right?"

"But, but..."

"Get a grip, Hanabi." She put her hands on Hanabi's shoulders, her knee on the bed, letting the crutches fall to the floor. "Get a grip, Suzuka Hanabi!" she yelled. "Are you or are you not a Motegi?!"

"Huh...?" Startled, Hanabi let out a strange noise. Rin ignored her. She took a deep breath.

"Listen! Suzuka Hachishiki probably thinks you're the last girl he saved or some trumped-up bullshit like that! But Okegawa Kuon doesn't think like that, does he? 'Oh, the Hero didn't need me, he didn't trust me!' Who cares? That boy isn't Suzuka Hachishiki! He's Okegawa Kuon! And Kyuu-kun is totally in love with you! Anyone can see he'd straight-up die for you! Otherwise, he'd never have pulled off what he did to save you back at the Capital! Come the hell on, Hanabi! Maybe his anger got the best

of him and he reverted to Suzuka Hachishiki or whatever, but if you do nothing, he'll die! You've got to make him turn back into Okegawa Kuon before that happens! You don't want Kyuu-kun dying, do you?!"

"No...no...!"

"Then get up! Go save him! Got it?! You're the only one who can save Okegawa Kuon! You're the only person in the entire world who can do that! Kyuu-kun needs *you*, Hanabi!!"

"If...if he doesn't...?"

Rin scowled. "Hmm...yeah, well, maybe that's possible. I mean, he does tend to do everything himself."

"See! See?"

But Hanabi, there's only one thing to say at a time like this. Listen up. "That's not the point! What do *you* want? Forget about what Kyuu-kun thinks! Let me say it again! You don't want Kyuu-kun dying, do you?!"

"I don't want him dying...!"

"Then the answer is obvious! Whether he needs you or not doesn't matter! If you want to save him, go save him! That's all that matters! Go! Just like Kyuu-kun ignored what the head-master said to come save you! Now it's your turn to go save him! To hell with the Hero's self-sacrificing bullshit! That kinda Hero is long gone!"

"Rin...?" Hanabi asked, her head down. "What if I just really don't want to fight? What if I don't care about Kuon-kun anymore?"

Rin just smiled patiently. "Then I'll give up. And then I'll give

you a big hug. And thank you for all the hard work you've done this far."

"...Do that now."

"Okay."

As Hanabi cried, Rin wrapped her in her arms, stroking her head. "You work harder than anyone, Hanabi. You're amazing."

"...Mm."

"Whatever the subject or the lesson, you were always way better than me. I was so proud to have a sister like you."

"That's 'cause you never took them seriously."

"But I was better at sniping."

"Heh heh, that's true."

"Hanabi."

"Hm?" She looked up at Rin.

"If you really don't want to, you don't have to fight anymore."

"After that whole big speech, you're saying that now?"

"I mean, you just looked so sad! And it was real cute."

"You started with 'fight for us,' and then somewhere along the way you started asking what I wanted."

"You noticed?"

"Of course! I get it, Rin. I know I have to go get Kuon-kun. I know I'm the only one who can."

"Gasp," Rin said, like she was on stage. "Look what fate has in store for you!" They stopped hugging. Rin leaned back, they looked at each other, and they both laughed. "You okay now?" Rin asked.

"I'm good," Hanabi answered, and took a deep breath.

In.

Out.

Innnnn...

Ouuuut.

Then she opened and closed her hands several times and stared at her palms a moment. Those palms had gotten Kuon all excited when he saw them turning into the palms of a Fencer. Then she slapped her cheeks.

She was still scared. But Kuon was on the other side of that Gate. She was sure he was fighting.

I've got to save him.

This thought finally rang true. She could still fight. She was a Division 5. She was a Maneuver Cavalleria. She didn't want to give up on him.

She peeled back her sheets, getting out of bed and back on her feet. She looked down at Rin and said, "Thank you, Rin."

"Don't worry about it."

They high-fived each other, and then Hanabi left the med bay without looking back. Her stride was confident. No bluffing, no hesitating. Just Suzuka Hanabi as herself.

She cut a gallant figure.

_/////////⌐

With the Heavy Magic Engines stopped, the Kiryu was running on electrical reserves. Unable to move or fly, it was simply receiving electronic maintenance, more or less just sleeping.

In the *Kuou*'s storage bay, a little fairy hovered in front of the dormant Kiryu, her eyes closed. "I see."

It was En. They hadn't made it in time for the operation, but Nanahoshi Kaede had reached the ship at the same time as Motegi Rin. "So that's why you stopped Hanabi-sama?" En whispered, like she was talking to the Kiryu. Then she turned towards the entrance.

"En-kun, you've come?"

Suzuka Hanabi came into the bay, wearing her plugsuit. Hanabi looked up at the Kiryu and said, "We're headed out. I'm going to borrow her power again."

"Hanabi-sama, she..."

"Mm, don't worry. I know."

Hanabi turned and flashed En a smile. *Oh,* En thought. *Hanabi seems different, in a good way. Like she's finally loosened up...*

Hanabi powered up her Device, donned Reimei, and stood before the Kiryu's twin heads, rubbing them. The electric reserves gave the Kiryu enough power that this formed a magic link. "Can you hear me, Kiryu?" Hanabi said. "You know what I'm thinking, right? That's why you didn't approve."

During the Fukuoka Gate Battle and Operation Jave World Annihilation, Hanabi's connection to the Kiryu was severed. She'd been wondering why that was, but her earlier conversation with Tooka had given her a clue.

"There's autonomously intelligent growth-type—NSR-type—AI Device functionality incorporated into portions of it, so it is absolutely 'thinking.' Even if it weren't, I personally believe all machines have a form of consciousness. Spiritual, electrical, or magical."

Like En, the Kiryu had its own will and magic. It got those from its creator, Tooka, which meant...

"I know you stopped me because that's what Kuon-kun wanted."

The Kiryu *was* Tooka. She and Tooka felt the same way about Kuon.

"At Fukuoka, I doubted Kuon-kun, so you rejected me. At Aohime, Kuon-kun wanted me to stay behind, so you made sure the Gate closed without me. Right?" Across the magic link, a tiny, tiny light flickered like a star. She was sure the Kiryu had nodded.

Such a good girl, Hanabi thought. *I bet she likes donuts.* She summoned her courage and asked, "Do you hate me?"

Two flickers. That was a huge relief.

"Thank you. I love you, too. I can feel such strong, sincere magic from you. That directness is just like Tooka-chan."

This time it flickered once.

"I've got a favor to ask, Kiryu."

No response. It felt like it was waiting for her to continue.

"I want to save him." She could tell the Kiryu was listening. "I want to save Kuon-kun," she said. "I don't want to let my Hero die a second time. You feel the same way, don't you?"

There was a long pause, and then it flickered once.

"I'm going to be real selfish about it. Even if Kuon-kun said not to come, I'm going to ignore that and go save him."

Flick flick, flick. The star blinked irregularly. Hanabi smiled.

"Sure. He might...he might not choose me. But I don't care if he just tells me not to get in his way. Once I've saved him, we

can fight it out and forget all about it. And this time I'll win. Gotta get him back for the entrance ceremony." Hanabi took a deep breath. She kept her eyes on the Kiryu and leaned in close. "I want..." she said. "I want to save him. I don't want to let him die. So please, Kiryu. Lend me your power. Let me wear you once more."

The Kiryu did not respond. For a long time, it was silent, neither nodding nor shaking her off. Hanabi saw the link between them in her mind as just black, no stars twinkling at all. Eventually the electric reserves ran out, as if signaling an end to their conversation.

"Kiryu..." Her words hadn't reached it. Hanabi let her hand fall, on the verge of giving up.

But then...

"...Huh?" In her peripherals, to her left, she saw a dial twitch, rising from white to yellow to green to blue to purple...and from purple to the Red Zone, indicating full revolution. Before Hanabi's eyes, the Magic Gauge on the other side of their link switched from electric reserves to full power. The Kiryu fired its Heavy Magic Energy, waking itself up. The heads lifted up, looking down at Hanabi.

Let's go, its mechanical eyes spoke.

"You're sure?" she asked, stunned. "Kiryu?"

As if in response, it nuzzled Hanabi. Its twin heads rubbed against the sides of Hanabi's face like an affectionate cat. Then it lowered its heads to her feet, like a knight swearing fealty to a master.

Hanabi knelt and put her arms around it. "Thank you, Kiryu. Let's save Kuon-kun together."

En had been watching in tears. Now she yelled, "Then I'll come, too!"

"En-kun...thanks," Hanabi said, turning around. Surprised, she said, "I didn't know you could cry."

"If my emotional values go over a certain threshold, yes."

"I see. Well, glad to have you."

"Let's go, Hanabi-sama! Kuon-sama is waiting for us!"

"Yes, let's go."

Hanabi stood up. Three days had passed since Kuon and Tooka went through the Gate. They couldn't afford to waste any more time.

CHAPTER 4

Each of Us Is—

K UON WAS STILL FIGHTING, all alone.

He remembered eliminating three of the Queens and two of the lights in the disc Jave. He had long since given up counting mantas.

The fight was miraculous, like a work of art. He overcame numerous situations where he seemed certain to die. In this one long battle, Kuon had repeatedly obtained the kind of experience and inspiration one normally gained over a very long life. He realized that the ultimate art could affect the light of life without Division 5 power when he killed the second Queen. Shichisei Kenbu was a Fencing school for those without power, so it made sense, really. That realization allowed him to minimize the use of magic across all his arts. He had finally reduced his magic expenditure by 1 *kei*, and Kuon was sure he'd gone up a rank or two within his school.

He was even enjoying himself despite the rage and hatred fueling his swings, despite the number of monsters he'd killed, despite the fact that his death was looming ever closer.

It was like threading the eye of a needle. His body was always

on the brink of death. One false move and his life would be forfeit. No matter how much he reduced his magic expenditure, his focus couldn't last forever.

He'd long since lost track of time, but then it hit him: a multiple-choice problem. How could he dodge the disc Jave's light bullet cluster?

A) Use Shitotsu to eliminate them.

B) Use shukuchi to gain distance.

C) Leap over them with his thrusters.

He chose A. As he eliminated them, dozens of mantas came rushing in. The Queen Jave's bullets blocked his retreat. He realized he'd fallen for their trap. He decided to cut through all the manta and lunge towards the disc Jave. He used all the arts he could and avoided the Queen Jave's bullets before realizing that, too, had been a trap.

A swarm of mantas rushed him from above. There was not enough room for a single hair to escape unscathed. Hundreds of mantas all swooped towards him like fish trying to swallow up a single plankton.

Dodge! his instincts screamed, but he knew that was impossible. There was no way he'd make it. He stopped time with Tensetsu and looked in every direction, but all of them were filled with open manta mouths and terrifying quantities of teeth. One second from now, each part of his body would be torn away by a different manta. In that light, the manta on his right was unlucky. He'd already lost that arm.

As this thought crossed his mind, Tensetsu was running out.

No good plans had come to him. It seemed Okegawa Kuon's end had come. In which case, he might as well go out with a bang. He picked a very dumb plan—his final self-destruct art.

His master had said she'd be sad if she let a second Shichisei Kenbu student die. Would she forgive him? She'd probably kick him out again, but...he wished he could see her again.

Had Tooka finally woken up? He was going to die first, so if she activated a black hole Gate at the cost of her life, she wouldn't need to mourn him. Next time he'd be a better brother to her.

Hanabi-senpai.

He'd been trying not to think about her. Remembering her made him not want to die. What he'd done to her was awful. He hurt her by not telling her his secret, breaking his promise to be with her, and going off alone again. If they met again in his next life, he would have to find a way to make it up to her. No matter how many years passed, no matter the age difference, he would find a way to say "I love you" to her once more. She would likely call him a liar and refuse to believe him, but he'd do it anyway.

Hanabi-senpai...!

Damn. It was too late. He really didn't want to die now. He didn't care if she rejected him, he didn't care if she ignored him. She could punch him, kick him, stab him, kill him if she liked, but he wanted to see her again. He wanted to see her smile once more, see that bashful look on her face. See her mad at him. Hear her gallant voice. Hear her gentle, cooing voice. Have her cuddle up to him. Wrap herself around him. Kiss him. Rub his hair, stroke his cheek, feel her warmth on him.

Hanabi, Hanabi, Hanabi, Hanabi, Hanabi, Hanabi, Hanabi, Hanabi, Hanabi, Hanabi...!

A wish rose up from the bottom of his heart—*I don't wanna die!*—and Kuon hated it. How pathetic. The soul of his last life, the hatred of a Hero long since gone, had tainted him. It had driven him through the Gate alone like an idiot, and now he was stuck here screaming that he didn't want to die.

Don't be pathetic. Head up! Dignity till the bitter end! At least take these enemies with you! Give Tooka the best chance you can!

Kuon took a breath. He was staring death in the face, clinging to a desire to live, but nevertheless he chose the optimal path. In that sense, perhaps Kuon was the hero people said he was.

Which meant he was doomed to meet this fate. A Division 1 powerless hero rushing in for no good reason would inevitably die like a dog. In this world, that was the way of things.

Yeah, he thought. *In* this *world.*

Kuon's Tensetsu would run out, the enemy attack lines would pierce his body, and there way no way for him to avoid death. His future sight had shown him that. He had to accept it.

But Kuon had failed to realize one thing: he was not in his world.

Shichisei Kenbu: Soryu Ranbu.

He could not predict attack lines that came from the other side of the Gate.

Tensetsu released. Time resumed. The magic compressed within Kuon's frame was ready to run wild, just waiting for him to pull the trigger. The mantas' maws were almost on him, and he tried to pull the trigger, but then...

He heard something. He was sure he did. A voice from deep in his past, a young voice asking him a question. The voice he loved more than anything.

"Hero, are you gonna die?"

An instant later, two light bullets shot out of the pseudo-Gate that had appeared right behind Kuon, brushing aside all the Jave around him. In the blink of an eye, all the enemies were gone. *What?* he thought in shock. *How? How am I still—*

"I finally caught up."

The voice came from behind Kuon. Still unable to comprehend what had happened, he slowly turned towards it. There, he found his goddess, Suzuka Hanabi, smiling awkwardly.

"How could you leave me like that?" She pulled away from the Kiryu and put her arms around Kuon. "Thank you, Hero. I'm only alive because of you."

She'd finally said it, after so many years, after thirteen years. That's what it felt like.

Then she saw his right arm and her face crumpled like his pain was hers. "Sorry it took me so long, Kuon-kun."

He didn't ask why she was here. He was just glad to see her again.

The tears came gushing out.

The Jave reacted swiftly to these new reinforcements, and the deaths of their fellows at the hands of their magic.

Screeeeeeeeeeeeeeeeeeeeeeeeeeeeeeeeeeeeeeeeeee!

The Queens screamed, firing bullets wildly. They approached the embracing humans at terrifying speeds, and by the time the girl turned towards them it was too late to dodge. Even if she avoided instant death, the wounds would certainly be fatal, and they could have their way with her, draining her magic until she died.

"Hmph." The girl just laughed, wearing an indomitable grin tinged with disgust.

Before the Jave bullets hit home, they were deflected by a black membrane.

Huh? thought the Queens. *What the—?! No, we know what that is. That barrier is the final magic from the twilight of our technology. The same magic that was on the black egg that "doll" came on. How are they...?*

No. It didn't matter. They'd find out once they ate them and stole their memories. They multiplied rapidly in such a short period of time. A top-class meal had been born quite recently and then the next a few days after that! They would have no lack of food. No need to let this one go. If they crossed to the other side, there would be more humans than they could ever consume. They'd start by eating these two, along with the doll.

Yes, they thought. *Kill them, kill them, kill the humans. The humans used us to protect them from disaster, turned our fathers and mothers and sisters and brothers and sons and daughters into beasts! Not one of them should be left alive. Consume all the humans in all ages and worlds, in the past, present, and future, make them regret what they've done.*

Every Jave in the solar system screamed together at the two humans in the skies over the Capital.

Screeeeeeeeeeeeeeeeeeeeeeeeeeeeeeeeeeeeeeeeeeeeeeeeeeeeeeeeeeeeeee!!

Their war cry terrified all humans, without exception. But these two hovered in the skies, unflinching. The Jave instinctively understood that these humans could very well be their natural predators.

The Jave fired. Suzuka Hanabi and the Kiryu, connected by a magic line, deployed their Heavy Magic Field and watched as it deflected hundreds of bullets. "Thank you, Kiryu," Hanabi said, looking up. She seemed awfully calm.

It was strange. Despite their cries, she didn't feel at all afraid. She wondered if the fear was numbing her emotions, but she had plenty of those urging her to fight, so that didn't explain it. The Witch Bubble and Heavy Magic Field were certainly dampening the soundwaves, but she suspected the biggest factor was the boy holding her hand. "Strange," she told him. "When I'm with you, I'm not scared of anything."

"I feel the same way, Senpai."

"You do?"

"I do."

The Jave weren't moving. Were they working on some scheme?

Then a familiar Guide popped up right next to Kuon, surprising him. "Here we are in enemy territory, and you two can't stop flirting."

"En!"

"Nice to see you, too, Kuon-sama. Sorry we're late. I thought the only thing broken was your internal clock, but that arm...no, first let us carve our way out of this mess."

"Yeah... Wait, aren't you smaller than usual?"

He was right. En was usually the size of his palm, but now she was only half that big. "This is merely a satellite. My primary instance is still linked to Kaede-sama back on Earth. This one is linked to Hanabi-sama."

"Then we should call you En-chibi."

"Your flair for names remains the dumbest, Kuon-sama," En laughed. "No backup is coming. The Kiryu's output could only manage a Gate large enough for Hanabi-sama. For the moment, it's still open, and I'm linked to my main instance, but it will collapse momentarily."

"The Nürburg couldn't get the Black Hole Gate open, could it?" Hanabi asked.

"No, it couldn't. Tooka is likely still unconscious. The disc-shaped enemy has multiple lights of life, and rapid extermination is a challenge. If we don't wake up Tooka and open the black hole..."

"Hanabi-sama," En said. "Head for the Nürburg. Assess the condition."

"Roger that. What about Kuon-kun?"

"I'm ready any time, Hanabi-senpai!"

"Okay, then..." En said.

More bullets came at them. As they scattered off the Field, Hanabi merged with the Kiryu again, still holding Kuon's hand.

He connected the tail line, riding its back. Hanabi glared at the manta going into a wedge formation. "Lunatic Order, Fuji Squad! Double attackers, the Twin Stars, coming at you!" she yelled.

"Yeah!" Kuon yelled back, and Kiryu took flight.

Three Queens came at them from the fore while mantas swarmed on their right and left flanks. Kuon and Hanabi each took a breath.

"Shichisei Kenbu: Shijin Reppakuzan!"

"Twin Nova Launcher—fire!"

A red sword of light eliminated all three Queens, and the massive light beams fired by the twin dragon heads left not a single manta alive.

"Hanabi-sama! Nürburg below you on your right, on the surface, surrounded by enemies!" En cried.

The Kiryu pointed its head down. Over a dozen Queens and a swarm of manta were gathered around the Nürburg, and the two heroes lunged towards them without hesitation.

"Kuon-kun, time to try you-know-what out."

"Got it, Hanabi-senpai!" Kuon held his Blade aloft, and Hanabi put the Kiryu's engines at max revolutions. Their voices overlapped.

"Shichisei Kenbu!"

"Field at max!"

"Ryujin—Reppakuzan!"

The Kiryu became a dragon of red fire.

This technique was Hanabi's idea. Ordinarily, Shijin Reppakuzan gathered magic heat and turned it into the shape

of a sword. She suggested that instead of doing that, they use the heat directly. When Kuon said their frames wouldn't hold up to it, Hanabi added to her idea. What if it was outside the Heavy Magic Field? And what if they also added the heat used by the High Nova Launcher?

The resulting Twin Fire Dragon plunged towards the Nürburg from 20,000 meters above. It was enveloped by a Witch Bubble with a Heavy Magic Field over it, and on top of that, Reppakuzan's super destructive capabilities merged with the Nova Launcher's magic heat and wrapped around the frame, forming a dragon of light which vaporized anything that came in contact with it. The sheer volume of heat was so intense that the Kiryu's outline was imperceptible to the naked eye, as if the sun itself had plunged out of the heavens to destroy the enemy.

"Rahhhhhhhhhhhhhhhhhhhhhhhhhhhhhhhh!!"

With a roar, their Kiryu slammed into the clustered enemies. The mantas trying to break through the Heavy Magic Field were blown away by the shock waves alone, never even managing to touch the real thing. Over half the gathered Queens were instantly turned to mist.

That was just the beginning. The Kiryu immediately swooped up back through their formation and turned to target the enemy again. After the third strike, the dragon finally did a tailspin above the Nürburg, releasing the light. By then, there was not a single living Jave around.

"Hah...hah...hah... You okay there, Hanabi-senpai?"

"Ha-hah...hah...! Yeah, of course, Kuon-kun..."

The intense magic output and aerial acrobatics had left both pairs of shoulders heaving.

"Nürburg contacted!" En yelled. "Damage sustained! Tooka-sama's alive! Starting repairs and evaluation! The two of you protect it with your lives! Please! For the next thirty-three minutes, all our lives are in your hands!"

"Got it!" Kuon and Hanabi spoke as one while watching Jave gather from across the entire planet on their radar. The number of Queens alone probably numbered in the tens of thousands, and there were trillions of mantas. The disc Jave above maintained a sinister silence, but no matter how they looked at it, the two of them alone stood no chance of winning. Yet neither Kuon nor Hanabi were at all afraid.

Because Hanabi's here.

Because Kuon's here.

The Twin Star Heroes each took a deep breath and let it out slowly.

"Come at us!"

It was the longest thirty minutes of their lives.

In the first eighteen minutes, the Kiryu used up all the Mother Servant Pods, Nova Gravity Bombs, flash rupture wires, back torque limiters, and prominence gull arms, leaving it with only the main Twin Nova Launcher and the proximity Servant Blades. Even for a Division 5 like Hanabi, her magic was almost tapped out by the time she'd slaughtered a few hundred Queens, and her mental fatigue was pushing against her limit. After fighting alone

for so long, Kuon was in a similar condition. No matter how low he set his magic output, there was still a finite amount, and his missing arm often slowed his judgment.

Attacking tentacles while acting as bait for bullets and mantas, Kuon shouted, "En, how much longer?!"

"Three minutes, twenty-eight seconds!"

"Heh heh, so precise!"

"I am a *very* high-spec AI!" Since neither Kuon or Hanabi let their fatigue show, En answered cheerily, working as fast as she could. She'd identified inadequate magical compression as the cause of the activation failure. The Nürburg had substantial electronic protection, so hacking the main CPU was tricky. She was forced to enter through an external socket, secure a bypass, and inject a fake version of herself. While the security protocols were killing that, En then had to attack the main systems, wrest full admin rights, and fire the boosters to the engines running the magical compression.

It still wasn't getting her anywhere. Tooka had seen Kuon right before passing out, so she had not permitted self-destruct. With Tooka still unconscious, she might have to resort to a final solution, but she still had one trick up her sleeve. The problem was that the kick didn't have enough power, so she could redirect the anti-magnetic field engine's electric away from stabilizing the Field, and in another three minutes and thirteen seconds...

Just then, the disc Jave far above them moved.

Screeeeeeeeeeeeeeeeeeeeeeeeeeeeeeeeeeeeeeeeeeeeeeeeeeeeeeee!

Its form changed. It shifted from a disc shape to a sort of tower, then extended downwards into a T-shape, and the extended tower

part began crackling with electricity. Both Kuon and Hanabi realized that they couldn't ditch the Nürburg to dodge this. The Heavy Magic Field could defend against any light bullets—

Craaack!

With a noise like a lightning strike, something pierced the Kiryu's right wing, slamming into the ground below. It had penetrated the Heavy Magic Field. Buffeted by a tremendous impact and shock wave, Kuon managed to identify the attack and yell, "It's a railgun!"

The disc Jave had turned a portion of its own flesh into a bullet and formed an electromagnetic acceleration device to launch it. The Empire had developed technology to turn magic into electricity, too, but this was the first recorded example of the Jave doing so.

If it had been just a physical bullet, the Witch Bubble could withstand it, whether it was a railgun shell or a nuke. If it was a light bullet, the Heavy Magic Field could deflect it. But they had no defense against a physical bullet charged with magic.

"They've adapted to the Heavy Magic Field!" Hanabi moaned, purging the damaged sectors with a shudder.

"En!" Kuon yelled.

"Two more minutes!"

The disc Jave's tower was pulsing above them, taking aim. "Next shot's coming! Kuon-kun!" Hanabi yelled.

"Protect the Nürburg!" He activated Tensetsu and saw the enemy attack lines. They were going to miss.

Baaaaaaam! Whoooshhhhhhhhhhhhhhhhhhhh!

The railgun hit home just behind them, generating a massive shock wave. Where it hit, it left a crater so big the Nürburg could fit inside it. If that hit them head on, they were done for. The one saving grace was its low accuracy, but that was no reason to relax. The Nürburg was sitting immobile directly between the two shots. This was known as target straddling. The next strike would be a direct hit.

This technology! They really did used to be... Kuon thought, and shook away the distraction. "Senpai! I'm going to cut it down! You cover the Nürburg!"

"Go for it!"

The Kiryu took position directly above the Nürburg, and Kuon stood on top of it. Kuon had blocked several massive light bullets from the Queens, which traveled much faster than the railgun shells. But the reason a physical shell was so scary—

"Seriously...?"

The disc Jave was extending one tower after another, each one pointed directly at them.

"Shijin Reppakuzan!"

"Twin Nova Launcher!"

The moment they saw this, both abandoned their defensive stances, going on the offensive. Using nearly all their remaining magic, they managed to blow away a number of towers, but those that remained...

BAMBAMBAMBAMBAMBAMBAMBAMBAMBAM!

Kuon stopped time and looked at the bullet trajectories, but there were too many to handle. He and Hanabi estimated which

bullets would most likely cause major damage if they struck the Nürburg, chose to block those trajectories, and then prayed.

Kuon released Tensetsu. Bullets like the manifestation of death itself came thundering towards them, and they turned their Blades and Servants and even their frames into shields, guarding the Nürburg.

It sounded like the world collapsing.

"...Guh!"

Their ears rang. When they opened their eyes, their vision was blurred and dust clouds filled the air. Kuon found himself on his hands and knees. He'd been thrown some distance from the Nürburg. His remaining limbs, at least, seemed to be intact.

Hanabi-senpai!

"Unh..."

He turned his head towards the voice and found Hanabi surprisingly close by. The Kiryu was filled with holes, badly damaged. It stood immobilized with its back against the rubble, its belly exposed. Only its head managed to slowly swivel, pluck Hanabi out of its embrace, and lay her down by Kuon's side. Then it went still.

"Kiryu, thank you. I'm sorry. I'm so sorry." Hanabi stroked its face. She was uninjured, but out of magic, and too tired to move on her own. For the moment, she was safe.

"En...are you alive? How's the Nürburg?" Kuon asked. He feared there would be no reply.

"Thanks to the two of you, the Nürburg is not badly damaged. But..." En sounded deeply sorry. She was crying. "I'm sorry. I've lost my connection. I'll have to go in again."

"How long?"

"I'm starting over."

In other words, another thirty-three minutes, Kuon thought. "Right."

"Enemy forces are still gathering. The disc Jave is repairing itself, but it won't be long before it fires again," En said. Her voice was calm but choked with tears. She didn't sound like an AI at all.

This is how it ends, Kuon thought. He wasn't Suzuka Hachishiki, but it was time to go out with a bang. He looked at Hanabi lying next to him. "Senpai, will you stay with me till the end?"

"Of course I will. We'll be together even if it kills us."

He reached his one hand out and touched her cheek, using the last of his strength to kiss her. "I love you, Hanabi-senpai."

She looked back at him with tears in her eyes and said, "If this is it for us, will you at least call me by my name?"

The disc Jave above them was making towers again. Jave from across the planet were gathering around them, and the disc Jave was doing everything it could to ensure the destruction of its natural predators.

In the midst of all that, Kuon said, "I love you, Hanabi."

"I love you, too, Kuon."

The wish Hanabi had been nursing all summer was finally granted.

She looked up. The dust clouds were thinning, and they could see the pitch-dark sky above. The disc Jave's towers glared down at them, ready to finish them off. This was Hanabi's last moment, and yet... *Huh,* she thought. *That's weird.*

Only now did it strike her as odd. The damage Kuon had done was the equal of what Suzuka Hachishiki had done to the Queen Jave back in his time, but the disc Jave was repairing itself far too quickly. That Queen had taken thirteen years to recover. Thirteen years and it still hadn't been fully restored. Was that really because of Magic Dispersal?

Something tugged at the back of Hanabi's mind. Next to her, Kuon was compressing the magic in his frame, preparing to unleash it.

There were no Jave nearby. The disc Jave was too far above. Even if Kuon used Soryu Ranbu to cause Magic Dispersal, they'd barely do any damage. But it would at least buy En a little more time. That seemed like enough.

But only to Kuon.

Shichisei Kenbu.

Who said that? Kuon, Hanabi, even En all swore they'd heard a voice. Were they hearing things? This was the Jave World. Another world. There was no one else around them, and certainly no one else who could use Shichisei Kenbu, not here, not...

"Seven-count Strike."

Kuon and Hanabi couldn't see her. How could they? The Cavalleria was above the disc Jave, out of their line of sight. But even so, they saw.

Maybe it was a dream. Maybe it was an illusion. But they both saw humanity's strongest Cavalleria, seven wings of light at her back, a red sword of light in her hands. Both Kuon and Hanabi saw her plain as day.

"Shijin Reppaku Ryuenbu!"

A wind blew, and more than a wind. It was a storm, a tornado. A tornado-shaped blade of fire that cut through everything it touched and mercilessly melted the edges of everything it sliced, tearing through the heart of the disc Jave.

It didn't just pierce the disc. It ripped open a space so large it was like the hole in a donut. Kuon and Hanabi found themselves surrounded by a membrane of red light and realized it was protecting them from that incredible area of effect attack.

They truly saw her through the hole she'd opened. It was a little Cavalleria whose hair always turned red when her DM was deployed, someone Kuon knew better than anyone.

"Sorry I'm late, Kuon!"

It was Nanahoshi Kaede. Tears streaming down his cheeks, he yelled, "Master!"

"Jeez, you sure know how to worry people, you fool of a student! When we get home, you're gonna get a piece of my mind!"

"Yes! Totally!"

"Headmaster? But...but how...?!" Hanabi wanted to know how she'd even made it here. Only Hanabi could open a Gate, and just barely. Which meant...

"Oh, I see! Of course! Of course! That's how!" En suddenly got very excited. "That's why Kuon-sama and Hanabi-sama's clocks didn't match up!"

"My clock...? Oh...!" Hanabi exclaimed.

"Exactly! When I got here with Hanabi-sama, Kuon's internal

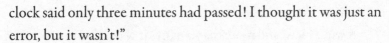

clock said only three minutes had passed! I thought it was just an error, but it wasn't!"

Kaede nodded. "Your real body noticed the same thing, En."

The little En yelled back, "The flow of time is different! One minute in the Jave world is a full day on Earth! Kuon-sama fought for three minutes on his own, while three days passed on Earth! Why it took thirteen years for the Queen Jave to recover last time, why enemy reinforcements only just started pouring out of the Gates back home, why it took Tooka-sama thirty years to be re-incarnated... This explains everything!"

The Queen Jave's thirteen years were only three days in the Jave world. The Jave had first appeared on Earth over twenty years ago, but even that was only a matter of days on their world. They had taken some time in this world to create Tooka, but far more time had passed on Earth.

"To the Jave, our world was an ideal environment that seemed to produce fresh food endlessly. We may only have one Division 5 every decade, but to them it seems like one is born almost every day."

"No, wait, En... How does that improve our situation...?"

The Jave clustered around them had seen the disc Jave's damage and were acting cautious, but once they'd appraised their strength they'd attack once more. Nanahoshi Kaede was unquestionably humanity's strongest Cavalleria, but she had a time limit—she could only fight for five minutes. It wouldn't be long before she ran out of magic, and then she'd be in the same condition as Kuon and Hanabi. They still had no chance.

Or so Kuon thought.

But En looked super pleased with herself. "Don't worry, Kuon-sama! While we fought for thirty minutes, over a month passed back on Earth! With that amount of time," she said as she spread her hands dramatically, "more than just Kaede-sama crossed over!"

Behind the little Guide's outstretched hands, as if responding to her signal, more Gates opened, one after another. Kuon counted them.

One, two, three, four, five, six, seven, eight, nine, ten, eleven, twelve, thirteen, fourteen, fifteen, sixteen...!

Twenty-eight Gates opened from the Earth to the Jave World, and what came through those Gates were...

"Kiryu?!"

An incredible number of Kiryu, even bigger than Hanabi's. Each dragon had three Cavalleria on board. A rider mounted on the back of the dragon's head, operating it, and behind them Attacks, Gunners, or Controls.

The swarm of Kiryu passed slowly over Kuon and Hanabi. These must be Alliance Cavalleria—they didn't recognize the majority of them. But Kuon did find a few familiar faces, and they waved down at him.

"You okay there, Okegawa-sensei?"

"Get hype, men! We get to save the Bushi Hime this time!"

"Can't let the assistant instructor hog all the glory!"

"Cavalleria!" A veteran called, clearly the one in charge. "Junryu Squads, attack!"

A roar went up from all quarters, and countless light beams shot towards the disc Jave. Heavy Magic Fields deployed as High Nova Launchers fired. These were definitely Kiryu. Their output was lower, and they likely took all three Cavalleria to activate, but they were still Kiryu.

Watching in awe as their allies fought the disc Jave in the skies above, Kuon sputtered, "But...but how...?"

"Mass-produced Kiryu. The Junryu, Kyuu-kun. Powered by three Division 4s."

Hanabi turned towards the voice and saw the Junryu rider speaking. Her jaw dropped. "How...?" she said and then swallowed the question.

"'Sup, Hanabi? You still alive there?"

"Rin! You came?"

"Of course I did! Our team's the ace of the Junryu Squad!"

The Control and Attacker behind her grinned awkwardly. "I tried to stop her, but she wouldn't listen. Glad to see you alive, Suzuka-kun."

"She wouldn't be a Motegi if she didn't come!" Another familiar voice spoke. "Oh, and Suzuka, Okegawa-sensei, you should know I joined the Fuji Squad."

"Fuji-kun and Okayama-kun!"

On the dragon's head, Rin puffed herself up, grinning. "Don't need both legs to fly, do I?"

Hanabi smiled through her tears. "Argh... You're all idiots...!"

It all fell into place. "I see," Kuon whispered. "You had the Crystal II and the Core with Tooka and Hanabi's data, so

if you could just get the frames, then a month was enough time...!"

These frames were why the Empire had been so hell-bent on getting the Capital back. With the Jave occupying it, the plans had been frozen, hidden underground. Nanahoshi Kaede had gone to the underground storage bays in the Capital to recover those units. The critical Heavy Magic Engines, like Kuon said, were reproduced using the Crystal II and the Core data. All they had left to do was place the engines in the frames. Their output was only half the Drag Ride's, but they didn't require a Division 5 to use. Three high-level Cavalleria would be enough to give the engine the kick it needed.

"High magic?" Kuon said. "Then not just Hanabi..."

"Exactly," his master said. The weapon on her back closed as she landed on the Fuji Squad's Junryu, glaring down at Kuon. "We no longer need a single Hero. Hmph. I'll give you credit for figuring that much out, at least."

"Now we don't have to make Hanabi do all the fighting!" Rin said, giving them a dramatic thumbs-up that was so like her. "Now, hurry up! While we're buying you some time!"

"Wake Tooka up, Kuon! I'm sure I taught you how."

En had joined them at some point. "Kuon-sama. Tooka-sama is not just asleep. She's retreated into her shell. At this rate, we'll never get the Black Hole Gate open. Come on!"

Kuon scrambled to his feet.

"You've got a way of contacting the inside without cracking the shell, right, Kuon-sama?" En asked.

Kuon had an idea what she meant. But... "I'd need magic equivalent to Tooka's, or..."

"You've got that! She's right next to you."

Oh. He looked at Hanabi. "Hanabi, lend me your power?"

She looked surprised and then made up her mind and nodded back. "Of course, Kuon."

He took her hand and pulled her to her feet, and they flew over to the Nürburg together to wake up their sister.

On top of the Nürburg once more, Kuon took a Blade from Hanabi and aimed the tip at his feet. His left hand closed around the hilt, with Hanabi's hands cupping it. He closed his eyes and took a breath.

Shichisei Kenbu Hidden 8th Form: Resonate.

Then he tapped the tip of the Blade at his feet.

Tiiiiiiiingg.

There was a faint noise. He pictured ripples spreading out, waves of magic entering the Nürburg, bouncing back like sonar. *Found her.* He'd caught Tooka's magic waves. He borrowed Hanabi's magic from the hands on his and let another set of ripples flow, contacting Tooka's waves. A moment later, Kuon's consciousness melted into the Nürburg.

Inside, Kuon's mind felt like it was sinking into the pitch-black depths of the ocean. When he reached the bottom, he found layers below him that were made of a gel-like sticky substance.

Inside that gel, at the bottom of the darkness, was Tooka. She was sitting, hugging her knees to her chest. He stuck his hands

into the gel, reaching for her, but she was just out of reach. Kuon called out to her. *Tooka!*

Tooka looked up, without expression. *Onii-chan, no. Go back. If you're here, I can't open the Gate.*

Yes. Let's open the Gate and go home together! You don't have to stay!

I can't go back. I'm not human. I'm a Jave. It's my fault everyone died. Tooka buried her face in her knees again. She was trying to punish herself for supplying the Jave with information and causing the deaths of countless humans.

That isn't your fault! The Jave did that! You didn't know!

It's the same thing. It's still my fault. I don't mind. I'm a Jave, so I'll die here with them. So... There was a thump, and the egg shook. Tooka had activated the Black Hole Gate. *Go home. You shouldn't get caught up in this.*

I'm not leaving you here!

I'm done. Just let me be.

His hands and words weren't reaching her. But he had to. Desperately, he called out. *If you die, Master...you know what it'll do to her?*

Tooka's shoulders quivered. *Mother...?*

Not just her! If we lose you, me and Hanabi and Squad Leader Fuji and Rin-san will all be sad, too!

As if realizing this for the first time, Tooka looked up, shaking her head. *That's...that's not...I don't understand. I don't know.*

That's what dying means! Everyone around you grieves!

But...but...!

He was crying now. Screaming. Suzuka Hachishiki's voice mingled with his. *I don't want to let any more family die! My family... They all died! I don't even remember what my parents looked like! The nuns who raised me, the friends I lived with there, the friends I fought alongside... They all died! I don't want anyone else to die! Please, Tooka, please! Don't die here!*

Tears trickled down Tooka's cheeks. *But I...I let so many people die...*

And you'll save far more! Your Kiryu! The Junryu! The Nürburg! The research you left will save the world! And if that's not enough, then I'll pay for it with you!

But...but I'm not human...

Who cares?! That doesn't matter! Kuon shouted as loud as he could. *You're my sister!*

But...but...Onii-chan, I...I just... She was sobbing now. The space around them was throbbing.

Crap, Kuon thought. At this rate, she was going to be swallowed up in the Black Hole Gate. *Give me your hand, Tooka!*

Onii-chan! Tooka reached a trembling hand up. Kuon leaned forward, desperately trying to grab it. Their nailed tapped, their fingers touched, their palms grasped. He had Tooka's hand in his. But...

Damn it!

The more he leaned forward, the more his body was swallowed by the egg. Tooka was in the bottom of a shell, deep in a swamp-like ooze that had swallowed her up. The more Kuon tried to pull her out, the deeper it pulled him in. He tried reaching out his other arm to pull himself up...

Shit!

But he didn't have a right hand. Kuon and Tooka both sank into the muck. Even his toes were growing cold, losing sensation. Tooka clung to his side, and he hugged her tight, trying to banish her fears. Then...

Jeez, you two. Trying to leave me alone again.

Something grabbed them both and yanked them up. Surprised, Kuon opened his eyes to find his goddess smiling at him.

I'm not letting you go.

Hanabi!

An instant later, Kuon's mind went white.

The disc Jave had been reduced to a tenth of its former size. On a Junryu above it, Kaede yelled, "Company Retreat!"

One by one, the Junryu Squads fled back through their Gates.

Kuon awoke to find himself held in the Kiryu's mouth, his arms around Tooka. Hanabi, of course, was flying it. He looked down and saw the Nürburg shining with a brilliant white light.

"Seven seconds to black hole deployment!" Hanabi shouted. She was headed for the Gate the Fuji Squad had opened. Rin and the others were on standby there.

"Hanabi, hurry, hurry, it's closing, get a move on, nowwwww!"

"Mantas approaching from below, on your seven! Okayama-kun, take 'em out!"

"Awright!" The Kiryu plunged into the Gate. Okayama cut down the manta on their heels, and Rin turned the Fuji Squad's Junryu into the Gate, but...

Screescreeeeeeeeeeeeeeeeeeeeeeeeeeeeeeeeeeeeeeeeeeeeeeeeeeeeee!

"Yiiiiikes, what the heck? They've come after us! Oh crap oh crap oh crap!"

The disc Jave had changed form again, thrusting out a massive tentacle several times larger than the Kiryu. It was like a wall chasing them through the Gate.

"Fly, Motegi-kun!"

"I aaaamm!"

Behind them, the Gate closed. A moment before, Kuon thought he saw the Jave World turn white, and it was probably not a trick of the eyes. The Black Hole Gate had opened. The magical black hole had swallowed up their world, destroying it. All they had to do now was finish off the massive tentacle Jave the disc Jave had sent after them.

"Someone do *something!*" Rin wailed, already flying as fast as she could.

At this rate they'd all end their lives here, inside this Gate. Kuon was at his limit, and Hanabi's Kiryu had sustained so much damage it was all she could do to keep it flying. Fuji and Okayama were shooting, but the puny rifles Control and Attackers wielded were useless against the sheer size of the thing. En popped out and started babbling in a very human-like fashion. "We're finally done for, we worked so hard, I hope it was enough, hopefully our next lives will be better ha ha ha ha wahhhh I don't wanna die!"

"Don't give up," someone said. The voice was calm but tinged with resolve.

Then two massive arms appeared from inside Kuon's grasp, palms forward. Exo-arms from a Division Maneuver. They had a second Division 5 with them.

"I want to live with you, onii-chan."

The massive, full-power light beam Tooka Nürburg fired swallowed the oncoming tentacle whole, evaporating it.

"Almost out!" Rin yelled. Their vision went white. Their long, short fight in the Jave World was over, and the Fuji Squad was home at last, back on Earth.

And back to Jogen.

DIVISIONMANEUVER

Epilogue

ALL GATES the world over had vanished. Every Queen that had opened a Gate and was lurking on the other side of it had perished.

There was some confusion.

A number of Queens had quickly opened Gates and fled to Earth to escape the Black Hole Gate, wreaking havoc as they took their last stand. The smart ones fled to Europe, which was still under Jave control, extending their lives for now. Some awaited destruction at the hands of the Alliance, while others opened Gates to other worlds and fled through them. It seemed there would be plenty of work for Maneuver Cavalleria for the time being.

The Empire was focused on clearing the Jave out of the territories where the Gates had been. There were still a number of Queens on the mainland, and it would take time to purge the last of them. To that end, the Empire elected to make a new military school on the southern islands—or, more accurately, reopen the old one.

Jogen Maneuver Academy may have been demolished in the attack, but it was open for business again.

It was December, one month after the Jave world had been destroyed.

There was one corner of the Jogen Maneuver Academy's grounds that had a cape that faced the Jogen ocean. On that cape stood a shrine to all the students who died in the school attack and during Operation Jave World Annihilation. The souls of all 376 lost slept here, watching over Jogen.

Fuji had begun spending more time alone and was even more focused on his duties. Sometimes he could be found staring blankly up at the sky. He hadn't quite broken the habit of choosing wedding dresses, but the occasions on which tears started flowing on their own were growing further apart. He intended to remain single the rest of his life but knew Nao would not want that, so for now he was left to wrestle with his emotions.

Rin's new right leg was artificial flesh, just like En's body. It was indistinguishable from her old leg, but magical enhancements made it extremely light, sturdy, and powerful, so she soon added somersault kicks to her repertoire. When she called it a "charge down into an up kick," Hanabi looked blank, but Okayama burst out laughing, so maybe he was the right boy for her after all.

Kaede formally adopted Tooka, who became a resident of

the Empire and had her name officially changed to Nanahoshi Nürburg Tooka. Tooka adjusted the Junryu until even Division 3s could pilot then, which mass-produced heroes. She then began working on research to prevent the opening of Gates from other worlds. She still lived at the Nanahoshi mansion, and when Kuon and Hanabi went to visit, she was very insistent they all bathe together, which was certainly alarming. She was apparently quite a fan of the Empire's baths.

This was all Rin's fault.

It was a sunny day at the Motegi mansion. A white arch had been placed before the stunning view from the second building, where they'd gathered for the fireworks. There was something church-like about it. Kuon stood in front of it, fidgeting in a white tuxedo. The fingers on his artificial flesh hand were twitching busily.

There were two benches in front of the arch, placed in a row. Fuji, Rin, and Okayama sat on one; Kaede, Tooka, and the large-sized En on the other. There was, of course, a red carpet rolled out between the benches, and walking down that carpet on Rin's mother's arm was, naturally, Hanabi.

Wearing a wedding dress.

A week earlier, during a squad meeting, Rin had suddenly said, "Hanabi and Kyuu-kun, you should have an engagement ceremony."

"Huh?"

Hanabi, Kuon, and Fuji all turned to gape at her. Okayama chuckled like he'd seen this coming.

"Kyuu-kun's still only thirteen, so an engagement's the best you can get. Let's do it at our place by the second building! Squad Leader, show Hanabi your folder of wedding dresses."

"I can do that, but..."

"Wait, wait, wait!" both Hanabi and Kuon protested.

"Don't get flustered in harmony! We're doing this!"

They had no idea what she was thinking. They never did, but still...really?

"Squad Leader, you're in, right? You wanna see these two engaged?" Okayama said, asking what no one else would have dared.

Fuji looked baffled that anyone was asking his opinion. "Wha—? Oh, I see. Right. No need to worry about me; I'll be fine. Actually, I think it's better to get it taken care of while you still can. And I genuinely want the two of you to be happy."

"Squad Leader approved! This means you've gotta do it. Right?"

"No, no, no, no, no!"

"Then it's decided! I'll call Mom and make her set up a church... Oh, this is gonna be so much work!"

The next week flew past in the blink of an eye, and now Kuon was standing there in a white tuxedo, facing straight ahead, waiting for Hanabi.

Hero, are you gonna die?

It was a strange feeling. The girl he'd saved shortly before his death in his previous life had become his fiancée in his new one. Was that how fate worked?

There was no telling when he'd die. Or Hanabi. From that perspective, Rin's proposal made sense. Like Fuji said, it was better to do these things while you still could. As those thoughts ran through his head, his white-clad bride reached his side.

The moment he laid eyes on her, he was sure that no matter how many lives he led, no matter how many times he was reincarnated, he would always find his way back to her.

Hanabi smiled. "Let's live together, Kuon."

She was the most beautiful girl in all the world.

Kuon nodded and then stretched himself up as high as he could and kissed her. He hoped that even if he someday grew to be as tall as her or taller, they would always be together.

The skies over Jogen were blue once more.

Several decades had passed since humanity's natural predators, the Jave, first appeared. They may have crushed their nest, but the threat of the Jave was still very real. The Maneuver Cavalleria had a long fight ahead of them...

But the Hero was no longer alone.

I'M NOT THE BEST with people; I've always kept them at arm's length, never been one to care about things outside my interests, and have worked with people for years without knowing how they feel or details about their lives (who they're in love with, which boss they can't stand, whether they're actually already married with kids) until well after the fact, and always find out about these things not from the person themselves but second-hand—which always makes me think, "Man, I should have talked to them more." But another part of me thinks, "Asking them would have been more trouble than it's worth," which leaves me shaking my head at my own lack of social skills. But still, a particularly vexing part of me is going, "Why didn't they just bring it up themselves?" Some things, you definitely want to know.

(Maybe that's just a long-winded way of saying I'm lonely.)

(Oh, well.)

BGM "Die Meistersinger von Nürnberg."

Hello and welcome. I'm Shippo Senoo.

My favorite ultimate move is Gunbuster's Super Inazuma Kick.

My favorite weapon is the Hummingroll's Black Hole Ocarina.

My favorite High Mobility Type is Black Sarena.

My favorite kaiju is Biollante, and my favorite ten thousand-fold is the Super X-II's Fire Mirror.

Well aware that I've now made basically everyone mad, from this point on it's time for the real afterword.

First, there's something I must tell you.

Division Maneuver is complete as of this volume. To everyone who read both novels of it, I have nothing but gratitude.

Genuinely, thank you.

I would have liked to write this until Kuon grew as tall as Hanabi, but this is out of my hands. At least I got to write that last scene.

In better news, like I mentioned in the afterword to the first volume, I also won a new writer prize from Shueisha's Super Dash Ex Bunko, and the work I won with should be published shortly before the release of this volume. And like I mentioned last time, there are a few small links between the two settings. That title (it's a long one) is *Though I Am a Terminal Witch, Is It Strange That I Am in Love Twice with Brother?* We're shortening it to *WitchLove*.

Certain types of stories have a main character whose role boils down to, "If it weren't for them, it would have been a tragedy" but I thought of both a success and a failure route, changed the time and place, and wrote two books—and they both won prizes at the same time, for which I am twice blessed.

At the end of this volume you catch a glimpse of the Jave's fury, and well, there you have it. If you're interested, give it a read.

Since this is the ending, I thought I'd go into the setting a little more. Think of it like a behind the scenes extra they do for movies. If you haven't read the novel yet, probably best not to read the rest of this. Unless, of course, you don't care about spoilers.

☆ **The locations of the Gates**—with the exception of Aohime Island—are all locations destroyed by a certain king of monsters: Sapporo, Sendai, Yamagata, Ashinoko, Owakudani, Mount Myoko, Matsumoto Castle, Nagoya, Kyoto, Osaka Castle, Seto, Hiroshima, and Fukuoka.

As a massive Biollante fan, I now feel I should have included Mount Mihara and Wakasa as well, but...at least I got Ashinoko in there.

☆ **Shichisei Kenbu's Hidden Eight Forms:**
    1st Form: Reject World.
    2nd Form: Bubble Wall.
    3rd Form: Crystal Cannon.
    4th Form: Foresight.
    5th Form: Void.
    6th Form: Pleiades.
    7th Form: Life Sight.
    8th Form: Resonate.
    Of these, the 2nd and 3rd Forms are the same as those that appear in *WitchLove*. There may be more.

Master Kaede can use the 1st, 2nd, 3rd, and 7th. She's basically a witch.

☆ **Queens live quite short lives and die after only ten years.**

☆ **The following are some mystery numbers** for those of you who haven't read the main story.

20 years=240months=7,200 days.

7,200 minutes=120 hours=5 days.

13 years=156 months=4,680 days.

4,680 minutes=78 hours=3¼ days. Essentially 1,440 times.

That's how I did the math. I messed up a bit along the way and the proofreader had to fix it, but let's keep that secret. They had really beautiful handwriting.

☆ **Sentences I had to cut for one reason or another:**

If asked why this school's girls' dorm had only female gorillas in it, the natural answer was "because it's a military school"—an elite one, at that, gathering only the strongest cadets the human race had to offer. The fact that Hanabi came equipped with a Maiden Mode made her rather an exception. Basically everyone else was pure female gorilla.

Humans born with a magic rank of 4 or above were mostly naturally beautiful, but since nearly all of them were either voluntarily or forcibly enlisted in military schools, after a year or so they'd all turn into unusually attractive female gorillas. If you turned a blind eye to the whole "cheating at mahjong" thing, Nao was a rare gentle-looking girl, and Fuji had done well to land her.

☆ **About Fuji-kun:**

He started out as a flawlessly handsome type, but this volume elevated him to co-protagonist in my mind. Seriously. The "flawlessly handsome" and "tragic backstory" combo is unbeatable.

What Nao said to Rin wasn't asking Rin to date or marry Fuji, just help him through everything as a friend. You know: "He's too serious, so help him relax sometimes." Or "Make sure no weird women get their clutches on him." That sort of thing. In fact, he's become quite popular with a certain type of girl, you know. "Ohh, he must be sad, but he never shows it, a flawlessly handsome guy with a dark side!" So we can certainly assume he has plenty of girls after him.

Finally, I'd like to thank my editor, Kurida-san; the illustrator, Nidy-2D-san; everyone involved in publishing; and everyone reading this book.

I pray that we will meet again in the near future.

Until then.

SHIPPO SENOO

A Libra, born in 1982. Began writing novels at the age of ten, jumped ship to screenplays, won an anime screenwriting contest and got a job at a game company, but still loved novels so went back to light novels like a total flirt. After four years of writing, he finally won and did so at both Kodansha-san and Shueisha-san's contests at once—a double prize! Pretty sure he's used up his entire life's worth of luck. He'll try to live strong.

NIDY-2D-

Illustrator. Primarily for games like *Phantasy Star Online 2es* and *Gunslinger Stratos,* but also TCG and light novel illustrations and designs. Particularly good at mechagirls—drawings of girls fused with machines.

DIVISIONMANEUVER